In one dreadful evening, Laura Bentley's world is torn apart.

"Aren't you even going to speak to me?" He reached for her arm.

She pulled her arm from his grasp and turned blazing eyes on him. "Were you speaking to me?" Her voice was like ice.

"Little Laura, what's wrong?" he asked smoothly. How could Laura have ever liked the sound of his voice? Now it sounded harsh and grating on her tattered nerves.

"I've just met your wife." How could she be speaking so coherently when her thoughts were so jumbled? . . .

"How could you think I would marry you? I won't break up a marriage, and I won't marry a man who is involved in this type of. . .business." Laura gestured toward the bar. . .

. . ."No!" Laura screamed as she covered her ears with her hands. She swayed as if she were going to faint, but two strong arms encircled her from behind.

LENA NELSON DOOLEY lives in Hurst, Texas, with her husband of 29 years, James Allen Dooley. *Home to Her Heart* is Lena's *Heartsong Presents* debut.

Home
to Her Heart

Lena Nelson Dooley

Heartsong Presents

This book is dedicated to James Allen Dooley, my husband for 29 years, who has supported me spiritually, emotionally, and financially—and filled my life with Romance.

ISBN 1-55748-451-1

HOME TO HER HEART

Tis the place that Nature picked
To dress in fine array,
Where people might forget all cares
And enjoy themselves at play.

Ah, tis the place of paradise
Especially in the spring,
To see the grass and blooming flowers
And hear the birds sing.

People come from miles around
To see the beauty there,
To tramp among the towering trees
And breathe the mountain air.

They climb the hills, cross the streams,
And camp along the way,
For it's a place of beauty rare
In this land of ours today.

If you have a yen for eating
Of fruits from off the limb,
As pears, peaches, plums, and apples,
It's there you will find them.

Perhaps you wonder if
You can find those fishing streams,
Of course, if you look for them.
They aren't just a dream.

So when you're feeling low in spirit
And need some relaxation,
Just pay a visit to the Ozarks—
The playground of the nation.

From the poem THE OZARKS, by Virginia L. Matkins Nelson, copyright 1944. Used by permission.

one

Although the day was sultry as Laura Bentley drove north toward her beloved Ozark Mountains, the heat didn't bother her. The top was down on her Thunderbird convertible, and the balmy wind felt almost cool against the nape of her neck where her long auburn hair was tied back. Laura was eager to reach her new home in a place that was special to her. Right after graduation from college, she had been offered a teaching position in the same town where she had spent her junior high years.

Although Huntington, Arkansas, might not seem very special to anyone else, it was to Laura. She loved the majestic mountains rising around the valley that cradled the little town. Of course, to be perfectly honest, the town had already outgrown the valley floor and now clung in picturesque clusters to the sides of both mountains. The mountain range intersected at the northern and southern borders of the valley, creating a pass at each end where the highway entered and exited. This created a feeling of isolation from the rest of the world, at the same time giving a sense of being part of God's unique creation.

Huntington held memories of the happy time when her family was complete. Laura's father had worked for the government, which required the family to move a lot.

They had lived in Huntington for three years while he did a study of the many polluted mountain streams which meandered across the slopes. Many times he had taken members of the family with him as he had gathered data. When Laura had been his chosen companion, she had explored the area surrounding each stream. She breathed in the fragrant spring lilacs and marveled at the rich hues of the autumn foliage. Even the humid Little Rock summers were forgotten in the cool mountain air. During the school year, the family's excursions were mainly confined to weekends, when the whole family enjoyed sliding down the snow-covered inclines on large pieces of cardboard. Her brother would always check outside the hardware store for used appliance boxes, which were far better sleds than any she had seen in catalogs.

As her car climbed the foothills, Laura slowed and switched off the radio. She wanted to savor the sights and sounds of the mountains. Although the dry summer had brought a miserable August in Little Rock, here in the mountains the trees were lush and green. Along the bubbling streams, even the thick undergrowth was verdant. The serenity of her beloved mountaintops always refreshed her, and as she looked for the signs of life she remembered, she felt that her heart was beating in harmony with God. Her years apart from these familiar surroundings melted away as she drank in the beauty of His creation—she was home!

A glance at her watch told Laura she was going to have to hurry to be in Huntington in time for her appointment with the school superintendent.

Although the past eight years had brought about many changes for Laura, she hoped the familiar town would be almost the same. Topping the steep pass, her heart leaped as she got her first glimpse of the town, looking much as she remembered it. Of course she could see that progress had begun to push clusters of homes and stores farther up the sides of both mountains, with a few glass-walled office buildings standing guard. But, however modern the town might have become, it still maintained the unique quaintness that she remembered so well.

As she pulled up to the administration building of Huntington Junior High, Mr. Tounsend was descending the steps to greet her. He watched as the pretty redhead stepped out of her car, looking like one of the students in her white eyelet blouse, green calico skirt, and white sandals. Her refreshing wholesomeness had impressed him the first time he had met her. Many of the young women he had interviewed for the position wore too much makeup, and their hairstyles were too sophisticated for the valley town.

His smile welcomed her. "You're right on time. I felt sure you would be." He reached out to offer his hand as she started up the steps to meet him.

"I always try to be punctual," Laura answered as they approached the door to the administrative offices.

"Isn't this a new building?" she queried as they walked down the hall to his office.

"Yes. Does the newness show that much? We tried to

build it so it blended with the architecture of the other buildings on campus."

"Oh, it does." Laura looked out the picture window overlooking the valley. "I just didn't remember it from when I was a student here. I love the view from this window. It shows the whole town. . .the whole valley."

"Yes, it does. We felt it was important that the entire complex take full advantage of the natural beauty surrounding it. I didn't realize you were a student here, Miss Bentley. When was that?"

"When I was in sixth, seventh, and eighth grades."

Mr. Tounsend ushered Laura into his office and showed her to a vinyl armchair opposite his heavy oak desk.

"Please make yourself comfortable, and we can discuss your duties. You know you will be teaching geography and history. You'll have one period of geography, two of American History, one of Arkansas History, and one of World History. That leaves you two free periods. I'll need you to spend one of them monitoring study hall, and the other you may use for planning and paperwork. And, by the way, I could certainly use your help in co-sponsoring one of our clubs. Since you are the first new teacher to arrive, I'll give you your choice of either Future Teachers of America or Future Business Leaders of America. What do you say?"

"Since I don't know that much about business, and I'll have my hands full with my new teaching responsibilities, I think I'll choose the club I know something about. I would love to co-sponsor Future Teachers of America.

Since for most of my life I wanted to be a teacher. I was active in FTA when I was in high school."

"Miss Bentley, why did you accept the position in our school system? Was it because you lived here before?"

"When I was a sophomore in college, my parents and brother were killed in an automobile accident," Laura started to explain.

"Oh, I'm terribly sorry, Miss Bentley," Mr. Tounsend was sympathetic.

"It's all right now, Mr. Tounsend. It was during that time that I really came to know Jesus. He carried me through the sorrow and pain and sustained me when I fell apart. When my parents were killed, my father was in debt. After all the bills were paid, there wasn't enough left for me to continue college. Because of my academic record, I was offered a scholarship from a private individual with the stipulation that I would teach where there was a need for a teacher in my field—but it had to be in the state of Arkansas. When this opening was presented to me, I agreed to take the job—if you would have me—even before I knew where it was going to be. It was an extra bonus to come to Huntington, but I would have gone anywhere to repay my debt. The fact that it's here was another of the wonderful things Jesus has done for me."

"I'm sure that's a commendable way of looking at it, Miss Bentley. Now we must take care of your immediate needs. I've reserved you a room for one week at North Mountain Lodge. It's new since you were here. The school will pay for one week, hopefully giving you enough time to find a permanent residence. You'll only be required to be at the school half days this first week, so you can spend the other time finding a place and settling in. By the way, my wife told me to ask if you would have dinner with us tonight. We'll be having a few of the returning teachers, too. This will help you get acquainted with your co-workers."

"Thank you. I'd like that very much. You've been so very helpful, Mr. Tounsend."

"Not at all. Would you like me to take you over to the Lodge, Miss Bentley?"

"No, thank you. I'd like to drive through town and see if any of the old landmarks are still around. I think I can find it."

"Okay. I'll call the manager and tell her you're in town and will arrive there later. I'll come by for you about 6:30, if that's all right with you."

"Of course. Thank you very much, Mr. Tounsend. I'll look forward to seeing you tonight and to meeting your wife and the other teachers."

As Laura left the administration building, she looked across the valley to North Mountain Drive trying to see the Lodge.

The town still centered around a delightful, well-kept park where she remembered hearing sunset band concerts and attending fall carnivals as a young teenager. She recognized many of the buildings, but most of the stores had either been redecorated or completely remodeled. She was looking forward to getting reacquainted with the town. Now, though, she needed to relax after her long drive from Little Rock.

As Laura's convertible scaled the narrow road along the side of North Mountain, she was surprised that she hadn't seen any large billboards announcing the Lodge, since it was relatively new. Rounding a curve and climbing even higher, her attention was drawn to the breathtaking view of the valley to her left. Returning her gaze to the road ahead, she caught a glimpse of sunlight reflecting on what appeared to be an entire wall of glass. The Lodge blended so well into its surroundings she had almost driven by it without realizing it was there. Instead of destroying the natural beauty of this mountain paradise for the sake of progress, the architect had designed the Lodge so that it almost became a part of the rugged landscape. The glass walls reflected the trees, cleverly camouflaging the beams that held the giant panes together. It was obvious that great care had been taken to disturb the native habitat as little as possible while building this magnificent structure. Laura was impressed.

As she pulled into the parking lot, she saw a rather portly man with a partially bald head step out the door. "Laura Bentley, welcome." He hurried to where she parked.

"Yes, but how? . . .Oh, I know, Mr. Tounsend said he would call."

"We've been expecting you all day, Miss Bentley. I'm Ralph Horn. My sister is the manager of the Lodge, and I help her in the summer. I'm also a fellow teacher. . . Computer Math. . .Let me help you with your bags, so you can rest before Mr. Tounsend comes for you."

As Laura followed Ralph into the Lodge, she realized the glass walls had been treated with something to make them reflective and keep those on the outside from seeing in. The lobby itself was a wonderful blend of lush foliage and cleverly arranged conversation areas, so that it gave one the feeling of having entered a private garden. The double stairway leading up each side of the main area formed an arch at the top of the two-story lobby. High ceilings gave the area a feeling of spaciousness that went well with the entire setting.

Since she was already registered, Ralph took her straight to her room. Laura stepped into a charming bedroom, divided into sleeping and sitting areas by a picture window looking out onto the breathtaking view of the valley below. As she began to unpack, she knew she would enjoy her week in this heavenly place.

Laura didn't like to keep anyone waiting. After she rested for a while, she bathed, dressed, and was sitting on one of the couches in the lobby watching the people come and go when Mr. Tounsend came for her. He pointed out places of interest as he drove her to his home. Several of the other guests had already arrived, so Laura was the center of attention when she and her host came through the front door.

"Let me introduce my wife, Linda." Mr. Tounsend indicated a pretty blond woman. "Linda, this is Laura Bentley, one of our new teachers."

"Welcome to our school, our town, and especially to our home, Laura." Linda's warmth bubbled as she held out both hands. "Now you must meet some of your fellow faculty members. This is Ralph Horn." She indicated the man Laura had met at the Lodge. "Perhaps you've already met him."

As Laura nodded, Linda drew her further into the hospitable family room. Margie Turner, the Home Economics teacher, was in her mid-forties with frosted hair and large glasses. Her husband, Henry, with coal black hair, towered over her. His rugged leanness broadcast that he worked outdoors.

Beverly Young, the senior English teacher was grandmotherly with her round figure and gray hair. Her friendliness and twinkly eyes gave Laura the feeling that she had known her all her life. Her husband, George, she told Laura, owned a dry goods store on the town square. Joyce Ramsey, a cute brunette with brown eyes, was the drama coach. She, like Laura, was single and had only been in Huntington one year. The last guest was Charles Hurd, the basketball coach and P. E. teacher. His blond hair, blue eyes, and ruddy complexion emphasized his rugged appearance. Heavy eyebrows shaded his eyes, and a thin scar started at his right temple and continued almost to the corner of his mouth. Instead of disfiguring him, it added character to his already fascinating face. Laura took one look at him and decided he was too self-assured for her, so she concentrated on getting to know the others.

Because she was having such a good time, the evening

was over before she realized it. Making a home in this town was going to be easy.

Mr. Tounsend was preparing to take her home when Charles offered her a ride, explaining that he was going by the Lodge to drop Ralph off anyway. There didn't seem to be any way out of it, so Laura agreed.

As they went out to the circle drive where the cars were parked, Charles led them to a two-toned green Chevrolet. When he opened the passenger door for Laura, she climbed into the back seat.

"I was going to ride in the back," Ralph said quickly.

"This is fine. You sit up there so you and Charles can talk," Laura declared sweetly as she leaned back on the soft upholstery.

Charles nodded and closed the door after Ralph was seated. He walked around the car and glanced quizzically at Laura in the rear view mirror as he backed out. All the way to the Lodge, he kept a conversation going with Ralph and completely ignored Laura, but she didn't care. She was enjoying the lights glittering like scattered diamonds across the valley. When they arrived at the Lodge, skillfully placed lighting illuminated the walls through the shrubbery surrounding it, making a wonderland of the landscape.

Charles reached for her hand to help her out of the car. Quirking one eyebrow, he looked her straight in the eye. "Miss Bentley, if you need assistance, please call on me." His confidence came through his touch and warmed her hand.

Breathing a quick thank you, she withdrew her hand and walked up the steps to the lobby without looking back. She was afraid to. She didn't want him to think he had made an impact on her. As she closed the door of her room and leaned against it, she wondered if she were making too much of what he had said. Maybe he only wanted to be friendly. He probably wouldn't think any more about her.

Laura didn't see the two-toned green Chevrolet lingering in the parking lot for ten minutes after she had left, or the puzzled look on the face of the man behind the wheel. Neither of them saw the grim look in the hooded eyes of a man standing in the shadows having a cigarette in the cool of the mountain evening.

two

Laura stretched like a sleek jungle cat before her eyelids fluttered open. What she saw startled her. Then she remembered where she was and basked in the mountain morning she saw through the wall of her room. The cerulean sky held cotton puffs of lazy, drifting clouds. The gentle breeze swayed the trees as birds flitted and squirrels scurried among the branches, oblivious of the people who watched them from the Lodge.

"Jesus, You've been so good to me," she exclaimed from a heart full of joy. "How can I ever thank You for all You've done?"

Laura leaped out of bed, filled with anticipation for what this new day would bring. Because she had this whole day to herself, she wanted to use it to get reacquainted with the town that would be her home for at least a year. After a quick shower, she chose a pair of teal blue slacks and a light turquoise gauze blouse. She brushed her long hair until it shone and tied it back with a scarf. When she fastened gold shrimp earrings and slipped into white sandals, she surveyed herself in the full-length mirror and was pleased with the effect.

Humming as she descended the stairs to the lobby of the Lodge, she felt again that she was entering a beautiful garden. When she reached the bottom of the stairs, she went to the young woman working the desk to inquire about a good place to get breakfast.

"Miss Bentley, your meals are included in your accommodations this week. There's a restaurant just beyond the elevators. Go in and order whatever you want."

"Thank you very much. But how do you know my name when I don't know yours?"

"We all know you, Miss Bentley. We were expecting you. My name is Susan Newby. I just work here part-time. I live on the road from the valley."

"I'm glad to meet you, Susan. I hope we'll get to know each other while I'm here. Right now, I'm famished." Laura started across the lobby toward the elevators.

She had just ordered a half grapefruit to be followed by an omelet when she heard someone call her name. As she looked up, she was amazed to see the mother of her best friend when she was in junior high.

"Mrs. Jackson, how did you know I was here?"

"I'm the manager of the Lodge. Please call me Rose now, Laura. I think you're old enough for that."

"Rose, how wonderful to see you. I'm so glad we'll have some time together. Where is Renae? Is she anywhere around here?"

"Would you mind if I join you for breakfast? I'll answer all your questions then."

"I'd be delighted."

Rose told Laura that her daughter, Renae, had married and lived in Huntington. Laura was excited. She hoped they would still have a lot in common and could continue the friendship started when they were young. They had lost contact after a couple of years of writing to each other.

"It's going to be hard for me to get used to calling you Rose instead of Mrs. Jackson, you know. It's not easy for me to break old habits, and you remember how much my mother stressed being polite to my elders," Laura smiled.

Rose laughed, "Thanks, but I'm not that old, you know."

Laura winced. "I didn't mean it to sound like that."

As she raised her eyes, her gaze wandered to a man framed in the entrance of the restaurant, and she could not look away. He was tall—so tall he seemed to dominate the room, though he hadn't even entered it. He was dark and his curly black hair tumbled around his brows. As his brown eyes bore into hers, she sensed that there was something familiar about them. She couldn't imagine why.

"Laura Bentley!" He started across the dining room. "It can't possibly be the Laura Bentley I knew as a freckle-faced teenager, can it?"

Laura was dumbfounded. Who could this man be, and how did he know her?

"Don't you even remember me?" His voice held a hint of mischief as he approached their table.

"Well, you do look familiar." She still was puzzled.

"You remember Gerald Eads, don't you, Laura?" Rose rescued her as he pulled out a chair and sat down.

A soft blush began at the base of Laura's neck and soon spread to her hairline. Of course, she remembered Gerald.

She hoped he didn't recall the last time they had been together. By the humorous glint in his eyes, she felt sure that he did.

She had been fourteen and had had a crush on the "older" man who drove her bus—nineteen-year-old Gerald Eads. He had asked her to go riding in his convertible the day of her eighth grade graduation. Excited and eager, she agreed. They drove up the winding road to the lookout tower. There he stopped the car. Her heart throbbed in her throat. His smooth voice began to tell her how beautiful she was. A blush had stained her cheeks then, too. She had been lost in the depths of those dark eyes and the sound of that silky voice. She shivered with excitement as he slid his arm across the back of the seat and dropped it around her shoulders. Tearing her gaze from his and turning it across the valley, she allowed him to draw her into a close embrace. When he asked her if she were afraid, she shook her head as she sank into the pools of his eyes. Her eyelids drooped as his lips brushed them. Her arms wound around his neck and she eagerly returned his kiss.

It wasn't the first time she had been kissed, but it was the first time she had enjoyed it. She knew by the way he kissed her that he was experienced, but she didn't care. She thought she was woman enough to be kissed by this man she had dreamed about for so long. He didn't press her to go beyond several delightful kisses, and she was glad because she was not at all sure that she would have been able to deny him if he had. It had been challenging enough to keep his hands where they belonged.

That same day, her father had told them his job was finished, and they were moving. She had never seen Gerald again—until today. Now he was sitting across the table from her, and all the things she had admired in him as a young man were enhanced by his maturity. How could she ever share with him the new dimension of her life?

"Yes, I remember Gerald. He drove the school bus I rode when I lived here before," Laura replied when she recovered her composure. "But, you've changed, Gerald."

"Laura, I would know you anywhere, but where have the freckles gone?" Gerald's eyes sparkled. "As I recall, you had a sprinkle of freckles across those ivory cheeks, didn't you?"

"Yes, but maturity brings many changes to us, don't you think?" was all Laura could manage to stammer, hoping he could see other, more important, differences in her.

"I would like a chance to discover all the changes for myself. Will you have dinner with me tonight?" Gerald's voice was still smooth.

Laura searched her mind for some way to decline, but she couldn't think of one good reason not to go. She agreed to spend at least part of the evening with him.

"I guess I didn't make myself clear. I want to spend the whole evening with you, helping you get reacquainted with the area. A lot has happened in this part of the Ozarks since you left so abruptly. It was eight or nine years ago, wasn't it?"

"Laura," Rose touched her hand. "I think you ought to go with Gerald. He doesn't live here now, but he spends part of every year here. He could help you see everything."

"I have an even better idea." Gerald didn't let her answer. "Why don't we spend the day sightseeing? We could let the evening take care of itself."

"I don't know." Laura hesitated. "I only arrived yesterday afternoon. I need to unpack and check out some things in town."

"That's perfect. I'll help you. I'll return for you in an hour. I won't take no for an answer," he added before she could protest.

As he rose to leave, Laura looked helplessly at Rose before she nodded her acceptance. She would go with him, and soon she would show him the real changes in her life. Laura couldn't help noticing how well his clothes fit him as he went out the door. His camel slacks had to have been tailored in order to fit his long, muscular legs, and his shoulders rippled under the smooth silkiness of his shirt.

Gerald was right on time. Exactly one hour later, he rang her room from the lobby. Laura was just starting out the door when the phone rang, so she soon joined him. As he looked at her, he sensed a difference in her. She had an assurance and confidence that he hadn't noticed in the restaurant.

"Where do you want to go first?" Gerald smiled down at her.

"I've only been to the school and to visit in Mr. Tounsend's home. What do you think I should see first?"

As Gerald took her arm to guide her to his car, he began

to outline an interesting day. When he opened the door of a silver Cadillac convertible with a red interior, she noticed how the car showcased his dark handsomeness.

"Gerald, this is quite a change from when I was here before, isn't it? You didn't drive a Cadillac then."

"No, life has been good to me. I'm sure you remember my family was anything but wealthy. I didn't drive the school bus because it was my hobby. Most of the circumstances of my life have changed in these last nine years."

"How is it that a man as handsome as you has escaped marriage?" Laura couldn't help asking as she glanced at his ringless left hand.

"Just lucky, I guess." Gerald laughed. "I've been too busy for any serious entanglements. Maybe that will soon change." His eyes glittered at her from the driver's seat.

"Don't look at me," Laura warned. "I'm not nearly ready to settle down. I still have lots of things to do now that I'm out of school and can afford to do them."

"Bravo!" Gerald clapped his hands. "You're a woman after my own heart."

Laura's breath caught in her throat as she again saw the view of the picturesque mountain valley. She would never get used to seeing it. Her pulse quickened, and she felt she had truly come home to her heart.

"It's awesome, isn't it?" Gerald saw the effect it was having on Laura. The two of them sat for a minute, drinking in the beauty, before he started the powerful engine and pulled out of the parking lot.

Gerald took her all over the valley and lower part of both mountains, stopping at intervals to point out the new additions he had mentioned. He treated her with respect, but in a relaxed way. She never felt, even for a minute, that she needed to be on guard against ideas that didn't fit with the lifestyle she had chosen for herself. Even though occasionally she felt the pull of a strong magnetism, she thought the fault was hers. She could see no indication that Gerald was trying to draw her to him. He was only trying to help her have a good time, and he kept a respectful distance.

As evening approached, he started up the highway that led northwest out of the valley. Laura glanced at him.

"Where are we going now?"

"I wanted to take you some place special for dinner. I remember you liked to go to the A. Q. Chicken House in Springdale. I thought we should see if they are as good as they used to be."

Laura turned to Gerald in astonishment. "How did you know I liked A. Q. Chicken?" she gasped in surprise.

"I heard you talking about it on the bus."

"But, how could you remember a detail like that for so long?"

"Laura, I've thought about you a lot during these years. I really wanted to get to know you better. We were making progress until you and your family moved. I couldn't believe my luck when I saw you at the Lodge."

"Gerald," Laura began hesitantly. "I need to tell you what's happened to me since we last saw each other. I have changed so much from the young girl you spent the afternoon with on the mountain. Although I was hoping you didn't remember that part of our time together, I figured you did. I was very immature then and knew little about men. You were the first man who kissed me and didn't disgust me. I'm glad you didn't take advantage of my innocence. . .but, I'm not that child anymore."

"Oh, I can tell that. Now you're an exciting woman."

"Wait, Gerald. I don't think you know what I'm trying to tell you. A big change has taken place in me. I've had a lot of hurts. My family is all gone now, except for my grandparents. During this time of grief, I came to know Jesus as a reality in my life. Now every aspect of how I live is governed by what I feel about Jesus. My relationship with Him will determine the direction of every relationship I have. It's only fair to tell you this. You may not want to continue seeing me under these circumstances."

"Laura, I remember the day on the mountain drive, too. I'm sure you are judging me by the boy who took you there. I just want to spend time with you and get to know you. Why don't we start over? I'll forget the girl on the drive, if you'll forget the boy. How about it?"

Laura's heart stopped its frantic flutter in her throat. It was not easy to talk to others about her deep relationship with Jesus. She was glad Gerald hadn't laughed at her.

"Gerald, are you a Christian, too?"

"I haven't been going to church lately. I did when I was younger, but I've gotten out of the habit. I don't think I know exactly what you're talking about, but I think I am a Christian."

Laura decided that would have to do for now. Maybe she would get a chance to share Jesus as a person later. Now she only smiled and enjoyed the scenery as they approached Springdale. The area had grown since she had last seen it.

Gerald pulled the sleek car into the small parking lot of the rustic building. "Well, here we are. Let's see if you like it as well as you used to."

When he took Laura's hand to help her out of the car, she noticed how other women were looking at Gerald. She should be proud to be seen with such an attractive man. One of his curls had fallen across his forehead, and it made him look even more intriguing. She decided to be glad he wanted to spend time with her, because he probably could have any woman he wanted.

The hostess could hardly take her eyes off Gerald after she seated them.

"Well, Laura, what'll you have?"

"What are you having?" Laura's father had told her to order according to what her date ordered. Then she would know she wasn't going over his budget. Laura mentally caught herself. How could she think a thing like that? It was obvious Gerald wouldn't ask a woman out to a place he couldn't afford.

"You can have anything on the menu." Gerald had read her thoughts.

"Thank you, Gerald. Old habits are hard to break."

After they ordered, they spent time getting to know each

other better. Laura told about the accident that had taken the lives of her parents and brother and about the hard time she had finishing college until the scholarship came through.

"By the way, Gerald, what do you do for a living?"

"Actually, I'm involved in several ventures. I own one restaurant among other things."

"Where is your restaurant? I'd like to go there sometime."

"Oh, it's in Fort Smith. I'll take you there," Gerald promised.

"I hope so. How can you be away for so long?"

"I'm on vacation for most of the fall, but I'm also attending to some other facets of my businesses. Actually, since I'm boss, I can be away any time I want to. I have a well-trained professional staff."

"How wonderful. . .Here's the waitress with our dinner. Did we really order all this food? I can't believe it."

"You eat a lot for someone so thin."

"It's just that this is the only place where I've seen French fries with batter, and they sounded good. I love the crunchy fried chicken, and I just couldn't resist homemade rolls with honey. I won't be thin for long if I keep eating things like this."

They enjoyed the food and very little of it was left when the waitress came to ask if they wanted dessert. Laura looked surprised, but Gerald ordered apple pie à la mode.

While Gerald was paying the check, Laura went to the ladies' room. As she was leaving, a woman at the other end of the mirror was staring at her. She just smiled and opened the door. She forgot about the woman as soon as she saw Gerald. He was holding a bottle of the salad dressing.

"I wanted you to have a souvenir of our day together."

"I thought souvenirs were supposed to be things to keep. This won't last long at all," Laura laughed.

As Gerald handed it to her, their hands touched, and she felt a tremor shoot up her arm. Her mind refused to accept it. She was not going to be the girl in the car on the mountain trail again.

On the way back to Huntington, Gerald kept up the light banter they had started in the restaurant. Because he could sense a subtle difference in Laura, he wanted to get her to relax again. He wasn't exactly sure what had happened, but he hoped he was having some effect on her. It was important to him that she once again felt relaxed and comfortable with him.

three

Laura's alarm went off at 5:00 a.m. She showered and washed her hair so it could dry while she had her quiet time with the Lord. As she took her Bible, she pulled a chair up beside the glass wall of her room. Since it was located on the east side of the Lodge, she could see the sunrise perfectly. She had just finished reading Psalm 91 as the sun peeked over the lowest part of the mountain. As she watched, the sky exploded with vivid color, driving out the muted tones of dawn.

"Oh, Lord, how can I ever thank You? You created a world so beautiful with gorgeous mountain sunrises and sunsets for me to enjoy. I thank You, Lord, for showing me what true love is. Your Word in Psalm 91 tells me that I never have anything to fear, because I dwell in You. Oh, Lord, protect me from any weakness my flesh might have. Thank You for Your love. . .thank You for my new job . . .and thank You for helping me this far."

Gerald was picking Laura up in time for the 11:00 service at the small church she and her family had attended. His offer to take her to church had surprised her. She didn't remember ever seeing him in church before. Of course, he could have attended worship with another congregation.

Laura stepped from the elevator, a shaft of sunlight catching the flaming lights in her hair. Gerald whistled his appreciation as she crossed the lobby in an emerald green sundress she had chosen with care.

Laura's eyes widened with pleasure when she saw him. The superb cut of his suit left no question that it was custom tailored for those broad shoulders and trim waist. He looked like he was going to an important business meeting, except that in his left hand he carried a small New Testament. Laura couldn't keep her admiration from showing as he took her arm and escorted her to the waiting car.

As they drove into the parking lot of the church, Laura saw Charles Hurd, the coach she had met at Mr. Tounsend's party, standing in the doorway handing out bulletins. He must be an usher. That meant he was a regular church member here. It was good to know there would be someone who wouldn't be a stranger to her. Hoping she would see some of the people who were members when she lived here before, she glanced around the sanctuary. A few faces looked familiar, but she couldn't put names with them.

Laura was deeply moved by the selection the choir presented. When the minister stood to share the Word with the congregation, she focused her attention on what he was saying. The preaching of this man impressed her. His sermon was solidly based on Scriptural truths. She had heard many ministers who quoted many sources other than the Bible. When the invitation hymn was sung, she decided to join. Fellowship with other believers had become an important part of her life, and she looked forward to becoming a part of this church family.

"I'm going to join the church this morning," Laura whispered to Gerald, and he made room for her to slip by him into the aisle. As he watched her walk down the aisle toward the front of the sanctuary, he puzzled over the change in her.

Full of joy and purpose, Laura walked toward the preacher. He was a fatherly man in his late fifties with salt and pepper hair and a twinkle in his eyes that told her he knew real joy. As he looked at the young woman walking toward him, he smiled a welcome. He was glad she was joining the growing church he had started pastoring only a few months before. Stepping forward as she approached, he took her hand warmly in his. As soon as the hymn was over, he introduced her to the other members and asked them to welcome her.

Laura was so happy, she didn't think about Gerald. She forgot he would have to wait on her until the church members were through greeting her. He moved to the back of the sanctuary, leaned one shoulder against the wall, and watched through half-closed eyes the smiles, warm handshakes, and the occasional hug Laura was receiving.

As the people who remembered her—and her family when they had been active in this church—greeted her, she was forced to repeat the news that her family was gone, but their sincere concern kept her from feeling sad. She also met many new people who were just as warm and friendly as the others. By the time all the people had greeted her, she had many invitations. The last person in line was Charles Hurd.

"I'm glad you're going to worship with us," he said with a smile. "How about coming to the evening service? I'd be glad to pick you up. After all, I already know where you live."

"I wouldn't miss it. I want to see if the evening service is as informal and comfortable as I remember." Just as she finished speaking, she felt a hand under her elbow and turned to see Gerald standing by her.

"I'm sorry I left you for so long," she apologized.

"That's quite all right. We won't be too late to get lunch at the Lodge Restaurant. If you'll excuse us," Gerald nodded to Charles as he escorted Laura out the door.

Charles's speculative scrutiny followed the two figures until they reached the luxury car.

As they drove into the Lodge parking lot, Laura turned to tell Gerald that he didn't have to eat with her.

"You aren't going to get rid of me that easily," he remarked before she could say anything.

"How did you know what I was going to say? Can you read minds?" she asked as she looked into his brown eyes. Then she realized why she usually avoided looking Gerald directly in the eyes. She couldn't stop feeling like she was drowning in the depths of them. They pulled her in like the vortex of a whirlpool. With an effort, she shifted her focus to the top button on his shirt.

"I just knew you would feel you are taking too much of my time." Gerald smiled as he noticed the effect he was having on her. It was only a matter of time before she would be eating out of his hand. "You are going to have lunch with me. We need to discuss this morning's service."

Laura was pleased that he wanted to discuss the thing that was so important to her, so she agreed to have lunch with him. After an interesting exchange, Laura invited Gerald to go to the evening service, too. She wanted him to share her love of Jesus and hoped it was an indication of his interest when he agreed to accompany her.

Charles and Gerald reached the desk at the same time and for the same purpose. The men acknowledged each other and walked away. Charles went to a phone booth and called the Lodge's number asking for Laura's room. Gerald circled around the lobby and asked the desk clerk to ring her room. When the phone rang immediately after she hung up, Laura realized what she had done. How could she have been so scatterbrained? Oh well, it wasn't as if she had a real date with either of them. They could all go to church together.

Smiling, she descended the stairs and approached first one and then the other. She told them her plan for all of them to attend church together. Charles was startled at first, but then he smiled and took her arm as they neared Gerald. Laura linked her other arm with his, and they steered him toward the exit. When she explained her idea, he went along with it. His plan could wait.

Laura enjoyed the evening service just as much as she had hoped. It was nice, too, that she could be escorted by two handsome men. Since Jesus had come into her heart, she had wanted to learn what Jesus expected from women and about Godly relationships before she pursued any entanglements. Maybe now she was ready to start dating. Hadn't the Lord brought two handsome men into her life in two days?

Laura couldn't remember when she had enjoyed a service so much. Besides a time of singing and praising, there was a time for testimonies—and the ones shared that night were a real inspiration to Laura. When the minister opened his Bible and began to teach from the book of John, she became completely immersed in what was being said. Her concentration shut out the people around her. She felt that the teaching was for her; when it was finished, she was renewed and strengthened in her spirit. When the last hymn was sung, she turned to each of the young men with her and smiled. Both of them could see the peace in her eyes, and it meant something different to each of them. Gerald didn't understand and vowed to find out what it meant. Charles understood and shared the feeling. Laura was not aware of either reaction.

"There's an informal social tonight in the home of one of the members of the singles' group. Why don't we all three go?" Charles looked first at Laura and then at Gerald.

"I'd love to go, wouldn't you?" Laura smiled up at

Gerald. "I want to get acquainted with the other singles in this church. And I just love socials."

"Of course, we'll go if you want to." Gerald turned to Charles. "You'll have to tell me how to get there."

Laura was glad Gerald was going. She wanted to see him in a social situation with Christians.

four

Monday was Laura's first day on her new job. As the car began to ascend the mountain drive that took her to the high school, Laura felt a few butterflies in her stomach. She told herself it was silly. After all, she had just spent four years preparing for this. She knew she was equipped to educate all the students entrusted to her. She told herself to walk in the confidence of Jesus. Since He had helped her receive her education, He would not desert her on her first day.

Mr. Tounsend had just parked his car as she drove into the teachers' parking lot. He smiled when he saw the young redhead emerge from her automobile. He gave himself a mental pat on the back for having hired her because he felt sure she would work out well.

Although Laura was a little anxious, she was also excited about her new job. There were so many things to learn about the school policies and rules. It was wonderful to be setting up her own room just the way she had envisioned it during the months since graduation. Because she knew exactly how she wanted it arranged in order to be the most conducive to learning, she was thoroughly prepared—she thought.

Just as she put the finishing touches on her new domain,

37

she heard the sound of footsteps. She turned, expecting Mr. Tounsend or one of the office aides who were already on duty to help the teachers. Her eyes widened with surprise when she saw the tall man with the probing brown eyes standing in the doorway. His silk shirt was unbuttoned at the neck, revealing a mass of curly black hair at the open throat. He certainly made an impact on her senses. Then she glanced at the dark eyes that looked intently at hers.

"Did I startle you, or am I finally making an impression on you?" His chuckle started deep in his throat and traveled all the way to his eyes.

"You've always made an impression on me, Gerald," Laura laughed. "It only surprised me to see you here."

"I wanted to ask if you would have dinner with me tonight. I'll have to be gone the rest of the week, and I wanted to see you again before I left."

"Well. . .yes, I'll go, if you really want me to. I didn't know if you would want to see me again after what I did last night."

"I enjoyed myself. Couldn't you tell?"

"Not really. I wasn't sure what you were feeling," Laura answered. "Come to think of it, I guess I didn't pay too much attention to you. I was so busy renewing old acquaintances and making new ones. I was having such a good time, and I didn't spend much time with you. Will you forgive me?"

"You don't have anything to apologize for." Gerald had moved across the room to where she was standing. His strong hands slowly massaged her tired shoulders.

"What time will you pick me up tonight?"

"Oh, I thought we'd go about 7:30. Is that all right?"

"Yes, but remember I'll need to be in bed early. I have to work again tomorrow. I'll see you at 7:30."

Gerald started out the door, then turned and waved, "7:30."

Laura stood staring out the door for a whole minute before she rubbed her temples. What was wrong with her? She couldn't get her mind back on the classroom. Maybe she was too tired to concentrate on what she should be doing. Mr. Tounsend had said her hours were flexible this week before school started, so Laura decided to take off early for a drive in the mountains, hoping to relax and clear her mind.

Within minutes she was sailing along the winding mountain highway, exhilarated by the wind blowing through her hair. As she sang along with the music on the radio, she was almost oblivious to her immediate surroundings. Rounding a curve, she saw a car stopped half in her lane and half on the shoulder of the road. She skidded to a stop, narrowly missing the stranded vehicle. Leaning her head on the steering wheel, she sat a minute to calm her nerves. Before she looked up, she heard a raspy male voice on her side of her car.

"Well, whut do we have here?" His speech was slurred. Her startled eyes encountered the face of a man she had never seen before. His unruly brown hair hung almost to his shoulders, and his beard was neither clean nor well groomed. The sleeves had been torn from his soiled shirt, and it was unbuttoned almost to the waist, revealing matted dirty hair and parts of tattoos—some of which were vulgar. His eyes had a slightly bleary look, as if he were either on drugs or a little drunk. It must be drugs, because she couldn't detect the smell of alcohol. As he turned to speak to his friend protruding from beneath the hood of the car she had almost hit, the friend looked up and smiled. Her blood ran cold as she saw the look in his eyes. He was tall and thin, and a rubber band held a long greasy ponytail that reached to the small of his back. A limp moustache hung from the sides of his mouth almost to his shirt collar, and his eyes were glazed.

"What'd ya catch, Elmer?" His speech was also slurred.

"Joe, look at her. I heard tell them redheads are a heap of fun. Maybe we'll get to find out. Come help me."

Laura was paralyzed with fear. Her mind couldn't accept what she was hearing. She hesitated for a moment too long. The heavier man jerked her door open and reached for her arm. Too late, Laura realized what was happening. As she lunged for the other door, his hand caught her sleeve and tore it.

"Looks like we got us a real spitfire, Joe. Come help me get her." By now the odor of the long unwashed body reached Laura, and her stomach began to churn.

As Laura opened the door on the other side, Elmer grabbed her arm this time. He jerked her back to his side of the car and then pulled her out of it. She almost lost her balance as her feet thudded to the pavement. Elmer jerked her against his filthy chest. The strong smell of his breath enveloped Laura as he leaned close to her. She shuddered.

"Joe, I think she just insulted me. She don't seem to want my kiss," Elmer said as Joe reached his side. "I think we ought to just teach her a lesson. Here, you hold her while I kiss her like a real man. Then I'll hold her fer you."

"This could get to be fun, Elmer, but just how come you get the first turn?" Laura swallowed the bile burning in her throat. She squeezed her eyes tight to erase the hateful scene, but she couldn't shut out the voices.

"Because I found her first."

As the two men began to quarrel, Laura saw her chance to escape. She ducked and broke the grip that had loosened slightly. She ran as fast as she could, but the tall man easily overtook her and grabbed her. Laura began to scream and kick. Her nails raked the side of his face, and she could feel the skin collect under them as she pulled them away. His yell sounded like a wild animal before it turned into a curse. He jerked her so hard she fell to the ground, but she never quit fighting.

"Hot dog, Joe, we got a live one. I always did like a woman with spirit." Elmer took her other arm and jerked her to her feet. "I'm really gonna show her a thing or two. She's gonna wish she'd given us that little kiss."

Laura's stomach turned as his face came closer to hers. She closed her eyes and began to pray. As she cried out to God, His peace flowed over her. Then she realized the men had released their hold on her arms. She opened her eyes to see the two men lying on the ground with another stranger standing over them. She could hardly believe her eyes.

"Who are you, and where did you come from?" she asked breathlessly as she looked at her rescuer.

"What are you doing out here by yourself?" The harsh voice sounded familiar. She turned to see Charles Hurd rushing toward her.

"I was enjoying a ride in the mountains to clear my head after a hard day." Laura was defensive. "You don't need to bite my head off."

Charles gently cupped her shoulders with his strong hands. "I'm sorry to come on so strong, but you gave George and me quite a scare. You should be glad we came this way from Fayetteville. There's no telling what this pair would have done if we hadn't come along when we did."

Laura turned to look at Charles's friend, who was standing over the two men crumpled into an unconscious heap.

"Did you get the sheriff's office?" George asked without taking his eyes from the two on the ground.

"Yes, someone's on the way."

Laura began to shake, and Charles pulled her against his broad chest. "Go ahead. Relax. Cry." Charles's hands were gently stroking her hair. "I went to Fayetteville to pick George up at the airport. I don't know why we took this route back to Huntington. We usually take the other highway." His soft murmur was interrupted by the sound of an approaching siren.

After the deputies took the attackers to jail, Charles introduced Laura to his best friend, George Hill, who was the Assistant District Attorney. He and Charles had been roommates in college and had remained best friends ever since.

"Miss Bentley, because I love these mountains, I'm working to help make them safe again. They're not as safe as they were when you lived here before. Please don't take a chance like you did today. You never know what will happen."

"I'm so thankful you two came along when you did."

Laura had been studying the man during this conversation. He was a little over medium height, and very muscular. His brown hair was in disarray and his hazel eyes held a look of concern. In his plaid western shirt and blue jeans, he didn't look like a lawyer.

"How did you overpower the two men who were attacking me?" she asked.

"They were so strung out on drugs, they didn't hear us coming. They were easy to subdue."

"I don't think I've ever seen anyone stoned in this part of the mountains," Laura said. "One of the reasons I love this part of the country is because it has always been so far removed from the evils of the big cities—or so I thought."

"Drugs are a problem everywhere," George observed. "It's one of the main projects we have in the D.A.'s office. We're trying to find the drug kingpin who is supplying the dealers in this area."

Laura glanced at Charles and found him looking at her

torn sleeve. "Oh dear, I must look awful." She tried to pull the tear closed with one hand as she smoothed her rumpled skirt with her other.

"Don't worry about how you look," George was gracious. "I'm more concerned about how you feel. We should take you to the clinic just to be sure you aren't hurt. I'm sure you're bruised."

"No, I'm all right. I just need to go to my room and rest," Laura replied confidently. Then she began to shake again.

"I don't think you realize you're in shock." Charles eased her into his arms again. Somehow those arms were very comforting. Laura's head nestled on his chest; and her shaking stopped.

"Why don't I follow you in her car?" asked George. "I don't think she should drive."

Laura straightened and pulled away from Charles. "Really, I'm all right. I've already been too much trouble for the two of you. I'll never be able to repay you."

"There's nothing to repay. . .and we aren't going to leave you, or let you drive home alone," George reiterated. "Since you already know Charles, I'll let him drive you ...and I'll follow. We want to make sure that you get home safely."

Laura didn't argue any more. Actually she was glad they insisted. When she rested her head against the seat, she knew she wouldn't have been able to drive home. At the Lodge, the men escorted her to her room and asked if there was anything else they could do for her. Then, they left her to rest.

Strong arms were restraining Laura, and she couldn't get free. The harder she struggled, the tighter they became. She twisted and turned to get away from the leering faces that kept coming at her from all sides. She wanted to lash out, but she couldn't. "Please," she cried. "Please. Don't . . .don't. . .I can't stand it." Then the most horrible laughter she had ever heard echoed around her as the faces came closer and closer. They were so filthy with unkempt hair and beards. She could almost smell the filth. . .almost but not quite. Why not? She squeezed her eyes to shut out the garish sight, but it didn't go away, so she opened her eyes. Where did they go? And what were they doing in her room at the Lodge?

As Laura shook her head to clear it, she realized that she had been dreaming. . .almost reliving the nightmare of the early afternoon. She must have slept fitfully, because she was wrapped tight as a mummy in her sheets. That was why she dreamed of being held so tight. After extricating herself from the confining linens, she stretched her sore muscles and decided to soak in a hot bathtub to relieve the soreness.

Adding a generous portion of her usually hoarded perfumed bath oil, Laura slid under the cover of the soothing hot water. Relaxing there, her mind returned to the surprise who took her mind off her work so much. She wasn't going to tell Gerald about her assault.

There was an air about him of barely restrained energy as if a cauldron were simmering and ready to burst into boil with only a spark. She knew instinctively that he was the type of man who wouldn't allow ruffians to mess with someone he was interested in.

When Laura was drying off, she noticed ugly bruises forming on her upper arms. As she explored the rest of her body, she found more bruises and a few scratches and scrapes. If she wore a jacket with the sundress she had chosen for dinner, they would all be covered. She probed each one and found some of them tender and others only ugly. As she was beginning to dress, the phone rang.

"How are you feeling?" a familiar masculine voice asked.

"I'm fine." Laura searched her brain for the name to go with the voice. She knew she had heard it before, but she couldn't remember where.

"Laura, this is George Hill, Charles's friend. I want to know how you really are."

"Oh, I knew your voice sounded familiar, but I couldn't remember where I had heard it. I'm fine. Really."

"You have been through a trauma. You may still be in shock. Are you hurt?"

"Well, I do have a few bruises, but I don't think any of them is serious."

"Did you get any rest after we left you at your room?" Concern colored his voice.

"Yes, I think I slept for about an hour."

"Look, Laura, I'm only asking you these questions because I need to know. Did you sleep well, or were you restless?"

"Now that you ask, I didn't sleep very well. I had

nightmares. Then when I woke up, I was sore; so I soaked in a tub of hot water. That's when I found my bruises."

"Would you let me take you to dinner?"

"George, how thoughtful. But I'm sorry, I already have plans for dinner."

"That's okay. Just be sure you don't do anything too strenuous. If you need me, I'm available. I've dealt with this type of thing before...and Laura, I hate to have to tell you this," George sounded hesitant. "...but you will have to talk to the sheriff sometime in the next two days. You need to decide whether you want to press charges," George continued as gently as possible.

"I have to decide?...I don't know what to do."

"Could you find time to talk with me tomorrow?"

Laura agreed to call George in the morning. Then she called Mr. Tounsend. When he found out what had happened, he told her she didn't have to come to school at all. The first teachers' meeting wouldn't be until Thursday morning, and she still had plenty of time to finish getting her room ready and prepare her first month's lesson plans before school started in two weeks. Just as Laura hung up, the phone rang again.

"Laura, this is Charles Hurd. I didn't want to bother you before. I hoped you were resting. I'd like to take you to dinner."

Laura couldn't help laughing. Suddenly she sensed a change on the other end of the line.

"I'm sorry I laughed. I wasn't laughing at you, but this is the second call in the last ten minutes asking me to go

out to dinner. I already told George that I am having dinner
with a friend. This is the first time I've ever had three
invitations for dinner the same night."

"Oh. . .well. . .I'm only sorry I was the third call. Do
we have to take turns, or will you have dinner with me
tomorrow night?" Charles asked jokingly.

"Yes. I'd love to have dinner with you tomorrow night."

"Good. I'll pick you up at 6:00." As the receiver clicked
in her ear, Laura realized how early that was.

five

As Laura stepped off the elevator, her glance swept the
lobby then rested on the man reading the evening paper
and standing near a beautiful palm tree. His burgundy
slacks and creamy silk shirt contrasted with the lush green
fronds. She was glad he was dressed more casually than
he was the last time they had had a date. Her pulse
quickened as he turned the page of the paper, and his
muscles rippled under the silk. Almost as if he heard a
sound from her, he turned and looked straight into her
eyes. His masculinity was overpowering. Taking a deep
breath to calm herself, she decided she had been more
affected than she realized by the incident that afternoon.

"You always look so beautiful." Gerald slowly surveyed her. "That particular shade of blue compliments
your coloring. What do they call it?"

"It probably has a more sophisticated name, but I call it
aqua. I wear it a lot."

"You might be too warm in that jacket, though. Why
don't you leave it in your room?" Gerald was reaching to
help her off with it.

"No. I'm comfortable." Laura straightened the lapels.

"Okay. Let's go. I'm taking you to Fayetteville for
dinner. There's a little Italian restaurant that serves the

best lasagna you ever put in your mouth. I'm hungry for Italian food. How about you?"

"Umm, sounds good."

As he opened the door, Laura wondered if she would ever get used to riding in a Cadillac. She leaned her head back on the velvet upholstery.

"Are you tired?" Gerald slid under the wheel. "You don't seem to be yourself."

"Yes, I'm tired. I guess it's the excitement of my first day at the school. I'm sure this evening will help me relax. I'll love riding through the mountains in a luxurious car like this."

Laura had meant it when she said it, but as they started into the mountains, her stomach knotted every time they rounded a curve. Her eyes scanned the road as if she were looking for something. She didn't notice Gerald watching her until his right hand took possession of her left one clenched on the seat between them. Instantly, she relaxed in his hold, and he loosened his grip.

"Are you going to tell me what's bothering you now?"

His tone was firm, but soothing and gentle. She knew she didn't have anything to fear from him, so she told him about the attack, trying to make it sound trivial. She didn't tell him about her conversation with George about drugs, because she didn't feel it was important for him to know. When she finished her story, she was sitting next to Gerald, and his arm was gently holding her close. At first she stiffened, but then she realized he wanted to protect her, and she relinquished her fear in his reassuring embrace.

"That's better." They had stopped beside the highway at a lookout point. "You don't have anything to fear from me. Have you cried since the attack?"

"No." Laura knew the one thing she wanted to do more than anything was cry. Gerald handed her a cream linen handkerchief and pulled her head to his broad shoulder. She began to cry gently. As he stroked her hair, the dam inside her broke, and she sobbed uncontrollably for what seemed like forever. Gerald continued to hold her, murmuring his comfort. His touch finally relaxed her. She sat for a few minutes snuggled in his arms with her head on his shoulder.

"I'm so sorry I've ruined your evening." Laura's voice had a catch in it. "I didn't mean to cry on your shoulder."

"My shoulders are broad; they can take it. Our evening isn't ruined. I'm still hungry for lasagna, aren't you?"

"I must look terrible. My eyes always get red and puffy when I cry. I need to fix my face."

Gerald cupped his left hand around her tear-stained cheek, "You look lovely. I don't think you could look any other way."

Laura didn't realize what he was doing until his lips found hers. She didn't have time to pull back before she felt the warm soft touch of his full lips. At first his kisses were feathery, soft, but then more firm. Before she could analyze her feelings, they were gone. His kiss had been gentle. . .and short. She didn't need to fear him. His kiss wasn't demanding like she had expected it to be. Maybe Gerald had changed during those nine years, too. She looked into his eyes without fear this time, and he knew it. He shifted position and started the car. Laura wasn't sure whether she was glad or disappointed.

The lasagna was just as good as Gerald had said it would be, and as they lingered over after-dinner coffee, Laura found renewed strength in his company.

When Gerald went to get the car, Laura stopped in the ladies' room. Just after she closed the door, it was jerked open by a very glamourous blond whose sultry eyes seemed to be blazing in anger. She stared appraisingly at Laura from head to toe and back to her face again. Laura couldn't understand the dark look—almost like hate—in those eyes. Laura was left to stand alone, confused and bewildered, as the exit door slammed in her face.

Gerald left the car at the curb and came inside to get Laura. While he was holding the car door open for her, her jacket caught on the edge of the door, slid off her shoulder, and part way down her arm. As she looked back, Gerald's gaze was riveted to the bruises on her upper arm. His eyes smoldered. Laura sensed tension in him like a spring that had been wound too tight. He pulled her to him and gently showered the ugly bruises with kisses. His ragged breath almost burned her flesh, and she was startled. At the sound of her gasp, Gerald seemed to take control of his emotions. He helped her into the seat and carefully closed the door. By the time he opened the door on the driver's side, his eyes were once again veiled.

"Do you need to go home now, or do we have time to do

something else?" he asked nonchalantly. It was almost as if the last two minutes hadn't happened. Laura decided to ignore it, too.

"I've had quite a day. I need to go to bed and rest."

"Are you going to work tomorrow?"

"No. I called Mr. Tounsend, and he said I didn't need to be at the school at all tomorrow. I'll have to talk to the sheriff, though. I probably won't have to be there until close to noon, so I can sleep late."

"I wouldn't want to take away from your rest, but I'm not leaving until mid-morning. Do you think you could have breakfast with me? Call me whenever you wake up, and I'll meet you."

"That would be nice. I'll miss you while you are away. How long will you be gone?"

Gerald looked deeply into her eyes. Again she felt herself being drawn by his charm. "Will you really miss me, Little Laura? I hope so." He pulled her to his muscular chest and gently, but firmly kissed her. It tasted every bit as good as it had before. She might like the chance to become addicted to those sweet, warm kisses.

In the morning, Laura remembered her promise to call Gerald. As she waited for his answering voice, she stretched, her body a painful reminder of the attack. She knew she would bear the physical marks for several days, and she was afraid she would carry the marks on her emotions for a lot longer.

"Hello. I hope this is who I think it is." How could a

voice sound alluring so early in the morning?

Laura couldn't resist the chance to tease Gerald. "And just who do you hope this is?" she asked with her voice buried deep in her throat.

"Don't think that will work with me, Little Laura. I would recognize the music in your voice no matter how you disguise it. How are you this morning, my sweet?"

Laura trembled from head to toe at those words. Did he realize he had called her that, or was this just his style?

"No, I don't make a practice of calling just anyone 'my sweet'," Gerald said as if he were reading her mind. "You're the only one. Now, answer my question. How are you this morning, or do I have to come to your room to see for myself? I've moved to the room across the hall."

"Why did you do that?" Laura gasped.

"So I would be close in case you needed something during the night. Now, are you okay this morning?"

"Yes, I'm fine. . .just a little sore."

"How are your bruises?"

"Oh, I think they'll be gone in a couple of days."

"Are you going to have breakfast with me?"

Laura looked at her clock and discovered it was already 8:30. "I couldn't possibly be ready for at least forty-five minutes. Won't that make you too late?"

"I'm my own boss. Any time I leave will be fine. I'll go to the restaurant to make arrangements for breakfast and be back to get you in exactly forty-five minutes."

True to his word, Gerald was at her door at precisely 9:15. He escorted her to a table set with silver, china, and crystal. Three pitchers were on the table. One held milk, the others orange juice and tomato juice. There was a pot of coffee, and steam was coming from the small vent holes in the tops of several covered dishes.

"My goodness," Laura exclaimed. "I've never had breakfast served this way. What's under all those silver domes?"

"Allow me, Mademoiselle." Gerald's gallantry was exaggerated as he held her chair for her. "I would have had it brought up to your room, but I knew you wouldn't allow me to share your meal there." His eyes sparkled with mischief.

When Laura was seated, Gerald swept the cover off the dish nearest him. It contained the most delicious-looking omelet Laura had ever seen. As he removed the other covers, the dishes revealed crepes, grilled Canadian bacon, and the last dish held an assortment of fruits and melons cut in bite-sized pieces. Then he lifted the napkin from a basket of croissants. "Your wish is my command. What will you have for breakfast, Little Laura?"

"Oh my goodness, I can't possibly eat all this," Laura exclaimed again.

"Laura, look at me." Gerald gently placed the index finger of his right hand under her chin and raised it until her eyes met his. "It's about time you began enjoying the finer things of life. You don't have to eat all this just because it's here. You choose what you want and eat that. Don't worry about the rest."

"I've had to struggle to get through college. I don't think

I would feel comfortable wasting all this food. . .unless you're very hungry."

"I think I can take care of what you don't eat today. It might be a long time before I eat again. So, Little Laura, relax, eat, enjoy." Laura watched Gerald put a small portion of each food on her plate. "Try to eat at least this much. You need nourishment after the shock you sustained yesterday."

As she began to eat, Laura remembered she had not asked the blessing on the last two meals she had eaten. When she looked up at Gerald, he was studying her. "What's the matter, Little Laura? Did I do something wrong?"

"No. I did. I'm used to thanking the Lord for His provision. I forgot it twice yesterday."

Gerald took her small hand in his large one and asked her to return thanks. They bowed their heads together, and she spoke a quiet blessing. Neither of them noticed someone watching them from a booth on the far side of the restaurant.

"How long will you be gone?" Gerald had to lean close to hear the soft question.

"I don't know exactly. I hope to be back by next weekend. I can't promise when, but can we do something together when I get back?"

"That would be wonderful." Laura's eyes danced with joy.

A new light was in Gerald's eyes, too. "Will you really miss me, Little Laura?"

Laura nodded just before his lips brushed hers. She was sorry the kiss was so short, but then she realized that they were sitting in a public restaurant. She started to say something about it, but his lips stopped her. This time, she relaxed and let him kiss her. It was the same sweet, soft, but undemanding kiss that she liked very much. He read this in her eyes and was satisfied. . .for now.

After Gerald took her back to her room at almost 11:00, Laura called George. She was ready to talk to him about her meeting with the sheriff. They made a date to meet in the lobby in ten minutes. Laura was waiting for him when he arrived. He took her to the booth in the restaurant where Charles Hurd was already drinking coffee.

As she slid into the other side of the booth, she sensed something disturbing in Charles' demeanor. She wondered what it could be but didn't ask. It really wasn't any of her business. She knew she had been mistaken when they first met at Mr. Tounsend's dinner. She no longer felt he was too cocky, and she liked being around him. After all, she owed her life to him and George. Charles looked at her with a question in his eyes as George asked her if she knew why she needed to talk to the sheriff.

Laura wasn't exactly sure, so George explained she needed to press charges against the two men who had attacked her.

"I never want to see those two again." Laura shivered as the two repulsive faces flashed across her mind. "Would I have to see them if I pressed charges against them?"

George reached across the table and took her hand. "You'll probably have to testify in court against them if you press charges, but do you want them to go free? They could do the same thing again. You wouldn't want that on your conscience."

"I'll have to pray about it."

Since he was a Christian, George understood. "Would you like me to go with you to the sheriff's office?"

"I want to go, too." Charles added.

That made sense to Laura. The two men were witnesses to much of what had happened.

"When will we go?" Laura asked.

"About 1:00. Would you like to have lunch with Charles and me before we go?"

"I'm sure she's not very hungry," Charles answered first, and Laura realized that his side of the booth had had a perfect view of her breakfast table.

"Have you been here long?" Laura was curious.

"Yes. I was waiting for George, and he was waiting for you to call before he came."

Why did he sound annoyed? Surely it couldn't be because she had had breakfast with Gerald. Then she remembered that Gerald had kissed her. Both kisses were short, so he must have been watching closely to have noticed them. Maybe he didn't like her to date Gerald, but she couldn't think of a good reason why not.

"I'm sorry I kept you waiting, but neither of you said anything about my eating breakfast with you. I had breakfast with a friend."

"Was he the same friend you had dinner with last night?" Charles sounded sarcastic. George looked puzzled.

"Yes. You know him. Gerald Eads. Remember we went to church together Sunday night. What's the matter? Don't you like Gerald?"

"Oh, I know Gerald. I've known him a long time. I can't say I don't like him, but he never struck me as a churchgoer before."

"Don't you think we should be glad he came to church? Maybe he'll come to know the Lord," George interjected.

"Yeah," Charles agreed. "Maybe he will, and maybe he won't."

"The Scripture says nothing is impossible with God. I, for one, am going to pray for his salvation," Laura asserted, hoping she didn't sound too sanctimonious. "You two order lunch while I go back to my room and get ready. I'll be back before you are through eating."

As she went up on the elevator, she remembered what she had just said about praying for Gerald's salvation. She needed to make sure he knew the Lord. She should have done that before she began to enjoy his company so much. He had been so gentle and caring, it would have been hard not to have had good feelings about him. That's all it was. She was grateful for the way he treated her. Then the vision of those dark eyes came into her mind, and she realized that it could be more than that. She was going to have to be careful. She didn't want their relationship to become serious before she knew for certain that he was a

Christian. How could she ever think about a relationship with anyone who didn't share her love for Jesus?

When Laura walked into the restaurant, George and Charles were just picking up their checks.

"Well, I couldn't have timed this better, could I?"

"No," George replied. "Finally our times are meshing."

The young men escorted Laura to Charles's car. This time when he held the door open for her, she sat in the front seat. He looked at her with a hint of laughter in his eyes and gently closed the door.

There was little chatter on the trip to the sheriff's office. Each of the three occupants of the car was lost in his own thoughts. When they arrived at the county courthouse, Charles let them out at the door and went to find a parking place. Laura was nervous as they entered the building, hoping she would not see the assailants. She was relieved when they were ushered into the sheriff's private office by the deputy on duty.

"Well, this must be Miss Bentley you're bringing in my office, George. I don't remember your ever bringing anyone so downright attractive before." The sheriff chuckled.

Laura knew he was trying to help her feel comfortable, and she appreciated it, but she wasn't sure it was working. How was she ever going to get through the next few minutes? She sat in the chair that was offered to her. She sensed rather than saw Charles enter the office and take the chair on the other side of her—and was thankful.

"I know you're a little uneasy, but just relax. I'm only here to help you, and you're here to help me." The sheriff smiled.

"Yes, Sheriff. I hope I can."

"Of course you'll help the sheriff." George was emphatic. "That's why Charles and I are here, too. We're going to give you whatever moral support you need."

"Now, Miss Bentley," the sheriff began.

"Please call me Laura. I'm more used to that," Laura said hopefully.

"Oaky. Laura. Tell me in your own words what happened yesterday. I'd like to get it on tape. Then I'll have my secretary transcribe it."

"Where do you want me to begin?"

"You may start wherever you want to, but you need to include all you can remember about the incident involving the two assailants," he said gently.

Laura closed her eyes and began haltingly to recount everything that happened after she left the school. It was easy when she was telling about her decision to drive in the mountains, but as she reached the part when she first saw the car stopped in front of her, she began to shake. She felt Charles place his arm around her shoulders, and George take her hand. She stopped her narrative and opened her eyes. As she looked at each of the men, her eyes expressed her thanks. She started the story where she had left off, but when she got to the part where the men began their assault, tears spilled down her face, and her voice was husky. Then she began to cry. She tried not to lose control, but the pain was deep, and it tore out in great sobs.

The sheriff came around the desk and also took her hand. He squatted on the floor by her chair and, in a very soothing tone, comforted her. Slowly her sobs grew quieter as she felt the compassion of the three men.

When she was able to continue, she finished the story as she remembered it as quickly as possible. As she finished, the sheriff asked if she were physically injured. When she told him about the bruises, he asked a woman deputy to take a look at them. Laura was taken to a private room by a young woman who was considerate of her feelings. When she had been examined and the bruises photographed, Laura was brought back to the sheriff's office where Charles and George waited.

She couldn't remember when she had been so glad to see a friendly face—except when the two men had rescued her. George and Charles were becoming important to her. It showed in her face as she entered the room, and her eyes quickly sought the face of Charles first, and then George. As her eyes returned to Charles's face, she saw something in his eyes she hadn't noticed before. She couldn't tell what it meant, but it made her feel happy and secure.

six

As the door to Laura's room closed behind her, she relaxed for the first time since she had entered the sheriff's office. She was glad the interview was over, and she wouldn't have to testify against the two men. When they pled guilty and received probation, they were assigned to a probation officer in their own county. The sheriff said they seemed genuinely sorry for what they had done. They attributed it to the fact that they were under the influence. Laura wondered why people couldn't recognize the dangers of drugs.

After several hours, Laura began to dream that the phone was ringing. She was trying to reach it, but she couldn't. Then she awoke to the realization that the phone was indeed ringing. She raised it to her ear, and her "Hello" was soft.

"Well, you are there. I was about to give up. I thought you had gone somewhere."

"No, Charles. I was asleep. It took me a while to wake up."

"I'm sorry I woke you because I know you need the rest, but I have some news. I talked to Mr. Tounsend, and he agreed to give the two of us one more day off. Would you like to go to the lake with me tomorrow and just play?"

"Oh my goodness. . .I don't know. . .I guess so."

"Listen, Laura. If you don't want to go it's all right. I just thought it would do you good."

"Oh, no, Charles. I'm just a little groggy. Yes. . .Yes! I'd love to go to the lake with you tomorrow."

Charles smiled at her exuberance. "Good. We'll make our plans over dinner tonight. I'll be by to get you in about an hour. George had to go out of town on some unexpected business. I hope you don't mind. We'll be dining alone."

"Of course, I don't mind. I'll be ready."

Why did Laura's heart skip a beat when Charles told her that? What was wrong with her? Why was this slight attention from a man making her feel giddy? It must be because of the emotional experiences she had been going through the last two days. Just yesterday, she had been affected by Gerald Eads, and today Charles Hurd was making her pulses race.

Charles had made reservations at a restaurant several miles away. It was located on one of the many lookout points. As Laura sat studying the view, she could see lights flickering over the valley. They were widely scattered, each one seemingly isolated from its nearest neighbor.

When the waiter arrived to take their order, Charles didn't even ask her what she wanted. He ordered for both of them. Laura couldn't decide if she liked that or not. He ordered things she liked, but probably wouldn't have ordered because of the price, but she wanted a chance to express her opinion. Everything must be catching up with her, and she didn't like the way she was feeling. She took a deep breath, closed her eyes, and relaxed. When she raised her head and opened her eyes, Charles was studying her.

"A penny for your thoughts," Charles whispered.

What a cliche! Laura thought. She was saved from answering by the arrival of their dinner.

"Madame is having the lobster?" The waiter set the plate in front of her.

"How did you know the lobster is for me?"

"Because Monsieur always has the Beef Wellington when he is here," the waiter answered smoothly.

Laura felt a blush creep up her neck, so she kept her eyes on the vista outside the window. Why did it bother her that Charles was a regular at this restaurant? She hadn't noticed until now that all the personnel greeted him like an old friend. Didn't they have the best table in the house?

"How did you know I like lobster?" She glanced at Charles a little peevishly.

"I heard you talking to one of the women at the Tounsends'." Charles smiled.

Laura didn't like to be patronized. Some of her feelings from the first night with Charles began to resurface. She ignored them and began eating the lobster. She hadn't had lobster very many times, but she liked it better than any other seafood—and she loved seafood. This lobster was the largest she had ever seen. As she took the meat from the split tail, she could hardly wait to get each bite to her mouth.

"Here's your butter to dip it in," Charles ventured.

"No thanks. I like the taste of the lobster too much to drown it in butter," Laura answered between bites. "I love the stuffed baked potato, too. I don't think I've ever had one quite like this."

"They use a blend of three different cheeses and whip it until it's light and fluffy. This is the only place I know that makes them like that, and I always order one when I eat here."

"Oh, do you come here often?" Laura tried to sound casual, but Charles recognized the undertones.

"Yes. It's one of my favorite places to eat. I've lived near here for years." Charles tried to match her attempt at nonchalance.

After dinner, Charles took her straight home.

"Get plenty of rest. We don't need to be in a hurry starting in the morning. Why don't you call me when you wake up?" Charles took her keys from her and opened her door. Turning toward her he tipped her face up with his right hand under her chin as his eyes searched hers.

Laura liked the look of gentleness in Charles's eyes. They had a kind of magnetism, too, but she felt comfortable instead of wary. Her imagination must be running away with her.

"I don't think I'll sleep very late. I'm looking forward to spending tomorrow with you." Laura watched Charles enter the elevator before she closed the door to her room.

Charles sat in his car outside watching the lights in her room. He spent many minutes praying for Laura. He knew she carried hidden scars from all that had happened.

When Laura hadn't called him by 10:30 the next morning, Charles wondered if she had changed her mind about going. He decided if she didn't call him by 10:45, he was going to call her. It didn't occur to him that she was still sleeping.

As Laura awoke to the sun streaming through the walls of her room, she stretched and lay there luxuriating in her leisure. She had fallen asleep as soon as her head had hit the pillow. As she noticed the sky out her window, she thought the sun seemed pretty high, but she still didn't think she had slept too late. She turned over and looked at the clock. 10:40! When she jumped up and dialed Charles's number, he answered on the first ring.

"You must have been standing right by the phone."

"As a matter of fact, I was waiting for a beautiful woman to call me."

"Well, I'd better hang up, so she can," Laura teased.

"Don't you dare hang up!"

"I wouldn't think of it. I'll keep your phone so busy she can't ever get through."

Laura liked the sound of his deep, throaty laugh. It sounded like it started all the way down in his toes and bubbled as it rose, causing her to feel light and happy, too.

"I almost decided you were going to stand me up today." He sounded serious.

"No. I just woke up. I must have slept over twelve hours."

"Good. You needed it. I hope it was restful sleep."

"Yes," Laura replied. "I haven't felt this rested in months."

Charles knew his prayers of the night before had been answered, and he breathed a prayer of thanks.

"What did you say?" Laura asked.

"Nothing. Now what time will you be ready to go?"

"That depends on what I have to do to get ready."

"All you have to do is get yourself ready. I've taken care of everything else. I thought we could go boating and swimming, so you'll need a swimsuit and whatever is comfortable. I'll be there in one hour."

As their car topped the mountain pass, the lake came into view. Laura had always loved the way the lake nestled between the mountains. The blue of the sky was mirrored in the smooth surface of the water. The surrounding scene was an artist's palette of earth tones, for indeed, an Artist had touched His brush to the earth. It was a special gift from her Heavenly Father right to her heart, and she reveled in the beauty of it. Charles watched her expressions without revealing his feelings. However, Laura was so lost in the experience that she was almost oblivious to the man who was riding by her side. She was in a world of her own, and it was a healing balm to her battered emotions.

As they neared the lake, Laura began to see some drastic changes since she had been there. "What have they done to my lake?" she asked almost defiantly.

"I'm sorry to say that progress is creeping into most of

the areas around the mountains. I don't like it any more than you do, but many people feel that it's worth it if it helps the economy. I have to admit that it has brought more money to the area."

"But, it's almost changed the character of the lake," protested Laura.

"I know, but we can still enjoy what God provided for us."

As they drove up to the new marina, Laura saw many boats moored there. Charles turned into the parking space by one of the medium-sized boats with a deep turquoise blue hull. The rest of the boat was white except for the gleaming brass fittings.

"Is this yours?"

"Yes. I can enjoy the water better when I can go anywhere I want to on the lake. The lake is over twenty miles long, but only fifteen miles are navigable. With this boat, I can go to the portion that is the least crowded on any given day, and I enjoy water sports. Do you water ski?"

"No. I've wanted to for years, but I never had a chance to learn."

"Well, we'll remedy that today. . .if you're game."

"Of course I'm game. When do we start?" Laura was delighted.

"Do you swim?"

"Yes. That's one of the things my father insisted on. Both of us kids had to learn to swim when we were very young. We used to live on War Eagle Creek directly across from a natural swimming hole. We just ran across the road and swam whenever we wanted to. There was only one swimming pool in town, and it was often crowded with the younger kids who couldn't drive. Most of the high school crowd came out to the swimming hole. It was an important part of my junior high days. I liked having older boys around. Of course, they never noticed Renae or me. We were too young, but we watched them."

"Were you really boy crazy?" Charles's tone mocked her.

"Aren't all junior high girls?" Laura laughed.

By this time Charles was ready to back the boat from its slip and head it toward the body of the lake. When he asked Laura if she needed anything from the store before they left, he told her they would lunch at the catfish restaurant on the island in the widest part of the lake. Since she had brought everything she thought she needed, he started the motor.

He skillfully maneuvered the boat through the crowded marina. When they were in open water, he opened up the throttle, and they skimmed across the top of the waves. The wind rushed around the sides of the windshield and tugged at Laura's long locks. They flew in the wind like a rippling flag. Charles could see that she was trying to gather them, so he slowed the boat. Laura was grateful as she pinned them into a bun on top of her head. Then she tied a scarf that matched her sea green short set around it to make it more secure.

"I really liked it the other way," Charles commented, "but I can see that it probably will be more comfortable for you this way."

"It'll be easier to comb later, too. It gets so tangled in the wind sometimes. I'm almost tempted to cut it."

"No! Don't." Charles's voice was almost harsh.

"Why do all men like long hair to be worn loose?"

"I don't know that all men like it that way, but I do. It looks like a living waterfall cascading down your back. That's what it makes me think of, a waterfall."

Charles was looking ahead watching where they were going, so Laura couldn't read his expression. He was glad of that. About that time they rounded a curve in the lake and entered another world.

"Where is everyone?" Laura asked. "It's as if all the boaters we saw on the other part of the lake disappeared."

"The tourists like the wider part of the lake we were in. Some who are more adventurous explore the inlets on the other side. Mostly only natives go the direction we're headed. It hasn't changed so much up this way. That's why I like it here."

"I'll probably like it better, too. I was disappointed that the lakeshore had gotten so commercialized back there."

The early afternoon was spent exploring. Occasionally they waved as other water lovers sped past, but for the most part, they were alone. Sometimes they rode slowly and marveled at the native foliage along the shoreline. Sometimes they rode fast with the wind blowing around them and felt like they were almost flying across the water. It was exhilarating to Laura, and she could almost feel the tension inside her melt as the spray showered around her.

In the early afternoon, Charles turned the boat toward the more inhabited part of the lake. They skimmed back across the lake, retracing their earlier route, and then they entered another narrow portion. Here they saw other boats constantly. As they rode farther and farther, Laura was puzzled by all the activity here. She didn't think it was any prettier than where they had just been. As they rounded a curve between two high cliffs, she saw the reason. Here the lake became even wider, and there was a fairly large island in the middle.

"I guess this is why most tourists go to this end of the lake instead of where we were," she ventured.

"Yes. The island has a beautiful beach on the other side, and the restaurant I told you about is here. Since it's after 1:30, I hope the lunch rush is over, and we'll be waited on quickly."

After they were seated in the spacious dining room, Laura was amazed at the variety of fashions she saw. She had slipped a matching skirt over her shorts so that she wouldn't feel underdressed. While many of the other customers were dressed in similar clothes, there were also people in everything from dressier clothes to cut-off jeans and halter tops with tire tread sandals. Laura couldn't help smiling.

"Can you believe all the different styles people are wearing? You'd think in a nice restaurant like this, everyone would dress up a little."

"I guess the management doesn't want to turn any paying customers away. Since this restaurant is on an island, all of the customers have gone to some trouble to get here, so I'm sure they take that into consideration."

"Well," Laura chuckled. "At least we are in the middle of the road—not too casual, but not too elegant, either."

Just then the waiter came for their order.

"I haven't even had time to look at the menu," Laura lamented.

"If it's all right with you, I'll order for both of us. I've been here before, so I'm familiar with what they have to offer. Do you like fried catfish? It's the specialty of the house."

Laura nodded as she thought about the difference between today and last night. He asked her opinion today. Maybe he just wanted last night to be special and knew she wouldn't have ordered lobster because of the price. She saw Charles in a different light.

"Do you need me to show you to the salad bar?" The waiter's voice interrupted Laura's thoughts.

"No, thank you. I've been here before." Charles escorted Laura to the largest salad bar she had ever seen.

"Are you sure catfish is the specialty of the house? Isn't it the salad bar?" she asked.

"I guess I should have said 'one of the specialties of the house.'"

"I could get permanently lost at this bar. I hope I can hold the fish when it comes."

As Charles and Laura returned to the boat, Laura commented, "All I want now is a long siesta. I feel like a stuffed flounder. I don't remember when I've eaten so much. You surely don't want to swim right now, do you?"

"No. I had intended to take you to visit someone who lives on the lake. This is a very special friend of mine. I think you'll enjoy her, too."

Without any further explanation, Charles maneuvered the boat out into the middle of the lake and headed back to the part of the lake where they had spent most of the early afternoon. Laura wondered about this "special" friend. Who was she? She began to have funny feelings about coming to the lake with Charles. Maybe he was engaged or something. Of course, there wasn't anything between Charles and her. He was just a friend, but why did she feel sad all of a sudden? She looked at him out of the corner of her eye, and when she did, she had a sinking feeling in the pit of her stomach. She didn't necessarily want a special relationship with him, but she didn't want him to be in a special relationship with anyone else. Now she began to wonder about her feelings for him. What were they, anyway? And why should she care about his relationship with someone else?

"Come back from wherever it is you've gone," Charles whispered into her ear. She hadn't noticed he was standing so close. How long had he been there? "Where were you anyway? You weren't brooding about all that has been happening to you, were you?"

"No." She turned and looked into those shimmering blue eyes. It was difficult to tell where the water and sky stopped and his eyes began; all the blues seemed to blend together.

"What were you thinking about? I sensed a sadness a few minutes ago." Charles casually—almost too casually—placed his muscular right arm around her waist and gently drew her to him. His other hand pulled her head to his shoulder as if he wanted to shield her. It was only then that she realized the boat had stopped.

For a long, satisfying moment she rested in his embrace. As his lips softly brushed first her hair, then her forehead, she closed her eyes. The soft warmth of his lips feathered down her cheek and touched her trembling lips. She enjoyed the gentle strokes before they settled more firmly. Without thinking, she returned the kiss, slipping her arms around his neck. She needed to hold on to him to keep her balance, not caring whether it was the sway of the boat in the water or her swirling emotions.

Then she remembered what she had been thinking about before he stopped the boat. She stiffened and drew away, and he quickly released her. His questioning look read wariness in her eyes before she could conceal it.

"Well, here we are. My special friend lives there." Charles pointed to a very old frame house, which looked as if it had sprouted up in the middle of a flowered carpet.

It was built of wood so weathered Laura couldn't tell if it had ever been painted. It was not exactly rundown, but it almost gave that impression. There was evidence that someone cared for it. By the porch, chrysanthemums in many colors grew in a flower bed bordered with rich golden marigolds. The flowers almost looked as if they were growing wild, because there was such a profusion of them. The windows and the door of the house were open, and lace panels fluttered gently in the breeze. The trees and brush had been cleared near the house, but there were only paths through them to the outbuildings behind the house.

Charles secured the boat to the ancient, but sturdy, dock and helped Laura out of the boat. He held her elbow impersonally as he steered her from the dock up the walkway to the house. As he stepped up on the porch, he called through the screen door.

"Granny, I've brought someone to meet you."

Laura abruptly turned to look at Charles. Granny? He had said, "Granny." Laura realized she had leaped to a wrong conclusion again. Would she never learn? That was a problem she had been working on for a long time. It had started when she lost her family and didn't have anyone to discuss things with. She had been used to doing that with her parents, and sometimes, even her brother. Their feedback helped to keep her on an even keel. Now she was always jumping to conclusions—many of which were faulty in some way. How was she ever going to tell Charles? Of course, she might not get a chance to tell him. He seemed pretty remote right now.

A small, spry woman came to the door and peered out.

"I was afraid my ears was deceivin' me. Is that really you, Chuckie? I ain't seen you in so long, I thought you'd forgotten me. I'm surely glad you ain't. Come in this house." Her eyes twinkled with her smile. As he entered, she disappeared in the bear hug he gave her. Laura felt like an intruder. "Who is this you brought? You ain't never brought a young lady to meet me. She must be special."

A blush crept up Laura's cheeks. Of course she wasn't special—at least not the way his grandmother meant.

"Granny, I want you to meet Laura Bentley, one of the new teachers at the high school. I'm showing her the sights. Laura, this is one of the really great mountain women, Granny Thrush."

Granny took Laura's hand in her bony one and peered into her blue eyes. "She looks like she'll be a good one, Chuckie. Set down and chat a spell. I'll just pour us some cider, and get some molasses cookies. The good Lord musta knowed you was comin'. I ain't made molasses cookies in quite a spell. They always was your favorite."

While she was in the kitchen, Laura studied the main room of the cabin. She didn't want to look at Charles. She had a lot of thinking to do before she looked into those blue eyes again, because they had definitely had an effect on her.

A large, oval rag rug almost hid the wooden floor. The furniture had seen many seasons, but it was not dirty. In fact, everything in the house was sparkling clean. The chairs and couch had crocheted arm and back covers in several intricate patterns, obviously handmade. The tables had doilies with high, starched ruffles. In one corner of the room, a bright handcrafted bag held yarn and the beginnings of a sweater on knitting needles. Several items looked like they were made from the sort of things Laura was used to throwing away. The room, furnished with homemade items, exuded a warm, lived-in feeling. On one wall were school pictures of children of many ages. Another wall was covered with school papers and drawings—some yellowed with age. Charles followed her gaze.

"Some of those papers are mine. I brought Granny one every year I was in junior high and high school."

Just then, Granny returned with the refreshments. She poured each of them a glass of cider and set the pitcher beside a heaping plate of cookies on the low table in front of the couch.

"Help yourself to the cookies and all the cider you want," she said as she settled in the rocking chair near the knitting and took the sweater on her lap. "Now, Chuckie, tell me all about what you been doin' with yourself, and tell me about yer new friend."

As Charles began to tell Granny about his summer, Laura relaxed. She liked the way he looked at his grandmother. Some men couldn't be bothered with elderly people, but Charles clearly enjoyed every minute of his time there. Laura was glad he had brought her, so that she could see him in a different setting. She had been completely mistaken by her first impression at the Tounsends' dinner, and she was ashamed. Sometime she would have to apologize to him not only for that, but for her mistake in the boat, too. She should have known he wouldn't kiss her if he were committed to someone else.

Both Charles and Granny were looking at Laura. "I'm

sorry. I haven't been listening. I'm afraid I was a million miles away."

"I hope you weren't out on the road to Fayetteville." Charles was concerned.

"No. I was just thinking," Laura answered, knowing he was referring to the attack.

The muscle in his jaw twitched as he told her in an impersonal tone that Granny had just asked her how she thought she would like teaching.

"Oh, Almost all my life I've wanted to be a teacher, and I worked hard to get an education degree. I have such high hopes for this year. I've always loved the Ozarks, so I couldn't be happier with my location."

Granny glanced over at Laura with a merry wink, and Laura felt accepted.

The rest of the visit flew by. Laura enjoyed the lively exchange between the two dear friends, and she participated in the rest of the afternoon's conversation with vigor. All too soon, Charles was bidding the older woman goodbye and promising to come again soon and bring the young teacher with him. Laura felt like family when Granny hugged her as they left. It was the perfect ending of an almost perfect day.

After Charles had the boat skimming over the water toward the part of the lake where he docked it, Laura looked at him and giggled.

"'Chuckie'," she chirped.

"What's so funny?"

"I didn't think you were paying any attention to me. I

only chuckled over her calling you 'Chuckie'. I suppose that started when you were a little baby."

"No," was his curt reply.

After a few minutes, he slowed the boat to a crawl and turned to her. "She isn't really my grandmother. I only met her when I was in seventh grade and was going through a very troubled time. My father was an alcoholic. When we moved here, my mother hoped he would quit drinking because this county and all those bordering it were dry. However, there were bootleggers here then. When my father drank, he wasn't any good. He was in and out of jail for public intoxication. It was difficult for my mother. She had to make a living for the family. She worked too hard . . .I didn't like what was going on. I spent a lot of time exploring in the mountains and got to know them like the back of my hand. During one of my explorations, I found Granny's cabin. She had been left a widow and was dirt poor. Her cabin was almost falling down around her, so I helped her fix it up. . .I learned a lot in the process. She kept me from rebelling and turning out rotten. . .I still check on her a lot. She has become the grandmother I never really knew. I try to see her every month, but this summer, I was gone a lot and didn't come often. She really let me have it for that, didn't she?"

Laura had been studying the emotions that flickered across his face. His eyes had had a faraway look as he talked. They only seemed to actually focus on her as he finished and caught her studying him. Their gaze locked for a moment; it was as if they could almost see to the bottom of each other's souls. It was a moment suspended in time and space. The mood was broken by another boat coming toward them too fast. Charles jumped to control the boat as they made a sharp turn to avoid being hit.

"Some people shouldn't be allowed on the water," Charles muttered as he guided the boat toward the marina.

When the boat was properly tied up, he helped Laura into his car and reached to turn on the car radio.

"This is K-O-N-E, the Christian voice of the Ozarks, where Jesus is number one. For your listening pleasure, we have 'Turn Your Radio On', by Phillips, Craig, and Dean."

"I didn't know there was a Christian station close enough to pick up. I tried to find one the first day, but I couldn't. Maybe they were having a newscast or something when I tried. When we get home, you can show me where it is on the dial."

seven

Laura awoke on Thursday with a feeling of great anticipation. It was the first teachers' meeting. She was anxious to get started being a teacher, and the meeting made it seem more official. She had been on an unanticipated two-day holiday. Now she wanted to get down to business.

She took great care choosing what to wear. Although a person's inner self is what is important, she wanted to project the right image in the teachers' meeting. She chose a deep rust skirt and short-sleeved jacket. With it she wore a sleeveless blouse in a muted peach, cream, and baby blue print. She placed her mother's pearl choker around her neck and added the matching pearl studs. Every time she wore them, she remembered the way her mother always bolstered her confidence whenever she needed it. Before rushing down for breakfast, she twisted her hair into an attractive chignon at the nape of her neck.

As she stepped from the elevator and turned toward the restaurant, she almost bumped into George Hill.

"What luck! I was just wondering about you, and here you run into my arms as I'm going to breakfast. Would you join me, or are you going somewhere else?"

Laura couldn't resist his infectious laugh, and readily agreed. She hadn't been looking forward to eating alone.

Mealtime was when she missed her family the most.

During their breakfast, George questioned her until he was convinced that she was really recovering from the ordeal she had been through. She told him a lot about the day she had spent with Charles at the lake. He tried to get her to eat a hearty breakfast to fortify her for her first day as a teacher, but she insisted on a light one, since she was more than a little nervous.

"You're eating like one of those girls who is always watching her weight. Surely you don't have to do that," he teased.

"Actually, I'm trying to be nice to the butterflies in my stomach," Laura laughed.

"You could've fooled me. You look calm and collected, and totally in control. Don't tell anyone. They'll never guess."

"Thanks. I needed that. Now, I've got to run."

When Laura reached the school, the teachers' parking lot was almost full. When she didn't see the green Chevrolet, she couldn't understand why she felt a sudden twinge of disappointment. Just as she approached the top step of the building, she heard a car enter the lot. As she turned and recognized Charles, she waved, but he didn't respond. She quickly entered the building, so that he couldn't see her expression.

She had been in her room about ten minutes when Mr. Tounsend and Charles knocked at the door and entered. Mr. Tounsend was carrying a corsage, and Charles was carrying a box.

"I always like to give the new teachers special recognition on the day of their first teachers' meeting. Since all the new teachers this year are women, I'm giving them a corsage. Really it was Linda's idea about the corsages, but that's one of the reasons I married her—her wonderful ideas. Charles was good enough to pick them up for me."

"And it wasn't easy getting them here without their being crushed. I had to watch them like a hawk all the way into the parking lot. It's a wonder I didn't have a wreck."

Laura looked at Charles to see if he were teasing, but he looked serious. Why did her heart suddenly seem a little lighter? Of course. He hadn't waved because he hadn't seen her. It wasn't anything personal.

"Thank you, Mr. Tounsend. I just love flowers."

Having completed their deliveries, the two men accompanied Laura down the hall to the meeting. When she entered the cafeteria with them, she was surprised at the number of teachers already there. She hadn't realized the school had grown that much.

She didn't know what she expected from a teachers' meeting, but it wasn't this. This was like a big fellowship group. Mr. Tounsend had each one stand and tell who they were, how long they had been there, and what they taught. He even asked them to tell what extracurricular activity they were going to sponsor that year. Laura was surprised when Charles said he was the other sponsor of FTA. She looked at him with wonder in her eyes, but he didn't seem to notice her.

After the returning teachers completed their introductions, Mr. Tounsend asked the new teachers to share a little something about themselves in addition to their classes. When it was Laura's turn, she looked straight at Charles as she said she had agreed to be the co-sponsor of FTA. He turned to the teacher next to him and said something. She wished she could have heard what he said, because the other teacher laughed.

Mr. Tounsend then gave each faculty member a copy of the school calendar and explained everything on it. Afterwards, he opened the floor for a brief question-and-answer period. He invited everyone to stay for lunch, because the cafeteria ladies had prepared a special meal for the teachers. This was a tradition that had been started by Mr. Tounsend when he had come to the school. It was good for the teachers, but it also gave the cooks a chance to prepare dishes that most of the students wouldn't eat.

Laura enjoyed the time of eating and getting to know her fellow educators. The new arrivals were soon made to feel welcome by their co-workers, and Laura appreciated their friendliness. It was almost 2:00 when the teachers began to drift back to their rooms.

Laura went to the kitchen to thank the cooks for the lunch. "I felt like I was back home at my grandmother's. That's about the highest compliment I can pay, because I've always thought my grandmother was the best cook in the world."

Laura returned to her room, but she couldn't concentrate on what she needed to do. As she went to the window and looked across the valley to her beloved mountains, her mind began to settle once again on the work at hand. She sat at her desk and worked out a schedule for Friday and next week. She wanted at least a month of lesson plans ready before the first day of classes.

With the schedule finished, she remembered she hadn't done anything about finding a place to stay when her week at the Lodge was over. She had accomplished all she probably could that day, so she went to tell Mr. Tounsend she was leaving.

After making sure she was showing no ill effects from her ordeal, he told her to take her time finding a place to stay. If she hadn't found a place by Saturday, they could extend her time at the Lodge since she had been through so much. She thanked him and left, her burden lifted and her step light.

As she drove through town, she remembered she hadn't tried to contact Renae. She would stop in to chat with Mrs. Jackson before going to her room to change. Rose was in her office talking on the phone, but she signaled Laura to stay until she finished. She had just taken the other chair when Rose hung up.

"Well, Laura, you sure do look professional in that very becoming suit. You have surpassed even my expectations for you when you and Renae were in junior high together. I'm proud of you. Your parents would be, too, if they could see you."

"Thanks, Mrs. . . . Rose."

"That's better."

"Okay. Thanks, Rose. I needed to hear that. It's times like this when I miss Mother. She believed in my abilities so much that she made me believe, too. That and my reliance on the Lord were the reasons that I was able to do what I did. And Mother always encouraged me when I needed it most. You sounded like her just then."

"I only said what I was thinking. I'm glad it helped."

"It did. . . You know, with everything that has happened to me, I haven't even tried to contact Renae. I really would like to see her soon."

"I talked to Renae today. She asked me to invite you to dinner either tonight or tomorrow night, if possible. Do you think you can make it either night?"

"Oh, yes," Laura replied eagerly. "I'm at loose ends tonight. Do you think it's too late to accept?"

"Renae's so anxious to see you, I'm sure it'll be fine, but I'll check just in case."

As Rose made the call, Laura pictured Renae the way she remembered her. Her dark blond curls just brushed her shoulders, and her blue eyes were so dark they sometimes looked violet. The last time Laura saw her, she was wearing her favorite dress—a purple-and-white print dress with a perky white sash. She looked very vulnerable. The tears welling up in her eyes emphasized their shade until they were almost the deep violet of her dress. Though she looked frail and helpless, Laura knew she possessed an inner strength, but it was being sorely tested now. Laura remembered her standing in the road and waving until they were completely out of sight. She kept seeing her like that for months after the move until finally she was able to recall their more happy times.

"Laura, Renae said tonight will be fine. Joe has a dinner meeting in Fayetteville. She's going to feed the baby and try to put her to sleep, so she'll be having a late dinner. She has asked me to come, too, so the three of us can reminisce. I hope you don't mind."

"Of course not," Laura insisted. "It'll be fun. It's exactly what I need tonight. What time will we be going?"

"How about 8:00?"

"Great. I'll meet you in the lobby."

When Laura reached the lobby, Rose was just getting ready to call her room. "It's about time for us to leave." She came toward the elevator. "We just have time to get there by 8:00."

"I'm sorry. I was going to rest a minute or two, but it turned into a long nap."

"That's all right. You needed the rest after all you've been through this week. Let's take my car, since I know where we're going."

When Rose pulled into the driveway of the red brick house built into the side of the mountain, the door was thrown open, and a young woman ran down the steps with arms open wide. As Laura emerged from the car, she was enveloped in a hug so tight she had trouble breathing.

"Laura Bentley! Let me look at you. Come into the house, so I can see how you've changed."

They walked arm in arm to the house. Laura could

hardly believe her eyes. What a contrast this self-assured young matron was with the fragile young teenager in Laura's memory. The violet-blue eyes were still surrounded by long, thick lashes, but the dark blond hair was now a soft beige. The dress she was wearing showed her now womanly figure to perfection. Obviously, having a baby had brought out the natural beauty of Renae's sweet spirit.

"Laura, I think I would have known you anywhere."

"Well, I don't think I would have recognized you if I had met you on the street."

Just then, there was a cry from the other end of the house. "Oh, no, I thought she was asleep." Renae started to leave.

"I'm glad she isn't." Laura followed her. "I wanted to see her. Remember how often we used to talk about getting married and having babies of our own? I wanted babies even more than you did. I've been looking forward to seeing your daughter."

When Renae turned on the light in the nursery, Laura saw a beautiful eleven-month-old child with tears running down her fat, pink cheeks. A halo of light blond hair swirled around her head and her blue eyes already had a hint of the deep violet of her mother's. When she smiled, her chubby cheeks dimpled on both sides.

"She looks just like you, Renae," Laura exclaimed.

"Well, at least she has Joe's dimples," Renae laughed as she gathered the precious bundle into her arms.

"Does she like strangers?" Laura sounded wistful. "I'd really like to hold her. . .if she'll let me."

"We can try. I'll take her into the den and let her get used to your being here. I'm afraid dinner will be a little late."

"That's fine with me. I'd rather hold a baby than eat."

When they went into the den, Renae sat with the baby on her lap. Before long little Josie was crawling all over the three of them. Rose offered to get the dinner on the table for Renae. While she was doing this, Josie climbed into Laura's lap and snuggled into her arms.

"She certainly is a good judge of character. She feels comfortable with you already."

"Good. I'll try to rock her to sleep."

As Renae and Laura sat and talked, Laura contentedly rocked the baby. Soon her little blond head became still as the feather-soft lashes fluttered shut. Laura continued to rock her until Rose had the dinner on the table. Laura couldn't remember when she had enjoyed anything so much as the feeling of the small warm body filling her arms. All the dreams of her early teen years came back to her. She wanted so much to be a mother.

Dinner was a joy. Renae and Laura did their best to catch up on all the time they had been apart. Laura told about the loss of her family and her struggle for an education. She also shared how Jesus had become a reality in her life. She was even able to share the traumatic events since she returned to Huntington.

Renae shared the story of how she and Joe had met and gotten married. She made it sound so wonderful, and it was clear that she loved her husband very much. Her eyes danced as she told Laura about how excited they were when they first found out that Renae was pregnant. Laura thought that being the mother of this precious little angel must be an incredible experience.

On the way home, Laura mentioned to Rose that she needed to find a permanent place to live, as her week at the Lodge had almost ended.

"Mr. Tounsend called and told me I could give you more time, and the school will pay for it."

"I know, but I really want to find a home. I hate to leave the Lodge, because I love the atmosphere, but I can't afford to live there permanently."

"Laura, I have an idea. We have some vacant suites at the back of the Lodge. They have a kitchenette and eating area, a bedroom, and a sitting room like an apartment. Sometimes our guests request a larger accommodation like this, but there is always at least one available. Sometimes I rent them to extra help we have in the summer season—at special rates for employees. I have been needing another back-up desk clerk, and you would be perfect! We wouldn't use you more than two or three times a month, and we could work with you on scheduling around your school activities. What do you say?"

"Well. . .it sounds wonderful, but it would depend on how much it would cost, and what they're like. Can you show me one in the morning?"

"Sure."

Before Laura went to school the next morning, she went with Rose to see the suite. Her decision was made when she saw the exquisite scenery visible from the large picture window in the sitting area. And, she reasoned, it was as private as any apartment would be, but she would feel the safety of having help nearby. If she wanted to cook, she would have a kitchen. If she were too tired to cook, she could stop by the restaurant for something. Since the price Rose quoted was within the budget she had allowed for housing, she decided to take it. She wouldn't mind filling in as desk clerk a few times a month.

"You can bring in any furniture you have to make it more like home. We can store any of this you don't want to use."

"I can't believe this is happening. It's definitely an answer to prayer. I'll tell Mr. Tounsend today that I won't need to take advantage of his kind offer, and I'll move in this afternoon." Laura hugged Rose before she left for school.

eight

Laura sat looking out the window of her room at the end of the first day of school. She was exhausted, partly because of all she had done that day, but partly because of the emotional letdown. She had spent the last week preparing for this day. She hadn't known exactly what to expect, but it certainly wasn't what happened. It had been hard to get the students to settle down even for her to make a roll. She heaved a tired sigh. She had had visions of being the essence of efficiency—a model teacher, and she was neither. Just then there was a knock at her door.

"Come in," she called, not too enthusiastically. "I'm not doing anything."

"I wanted to come and see how it went today." Joyce Ramsey breezed in.

Laura looked up and forced a smile. "Oh, it was just wonderful."

"Really? I remember my first day, last year, was a nightmare."

"Well. . .today was for me, too. I didn't get very much accomplished," Laura admitted ruefully.

"I thought so. I was going to educate the world when I entered the classroom for the first time. I soon found that there are victories and defeats in teaching as in any other field. Just because I was prepared to teach didn't mean the students were prepared to learn."

"I thought I would never get the kids calmed down. It took me almost all period to make a roll and seating chart."

"I didn't even try for a seating chart this year. You'll soon find they aren't very successful." Joyce chuckled. "Last year my third period class switched places every day for the first two weeks. I had a hard time learning all the names. I still call Jill Rankin, Judy."

Laura joined her in laughter. "I guess I was too serious today. I forgot what it was like to be a student. Maybe I'll loosen up a little tomorrow."

"Yes. Keep them off balance, and don't let them get to you. They should never think that they have the upper hand. . .You're looking a little more cheerful than you were when I came in, but you still need something else. Why don't we go out to dinner and celebrate the end of your first day of school?"

"That sounds like a winner. I was just going back to my apartment to feel sorry for myself. I don't need to do that." Laura started to gather up her books and put them in her tote bag. Suddenly she stopped. "Uh oh, I forgot. I have a date for dinner tonight. Could I have a rain check?"

"If that date is with a man, of course. I never stand in the way of potential love. Any time will be fine with me." Joyce headed toward the door. "Is it anyone I know?" She waited with her hand on the door knob.

"Do you know Gerald Eads?"

"I don't think I've heard that name before. Does he live

here?"

"No, but he used to when I lived here before."

Joyce looked puzzled. "I didn't know you lived here before. When was that?"

"My family moved away nine years ago."

"Well, you learn something new every day. See you tomorrow."

Laura was looking forward to her date with Gerald. He hadn't come back the week before, as he had thought he would. Tonight would be the first time they had been together since his business trip.

Come to think of it, Charles had made himself pretty scarce, too. She had seen him at church, and she had run into him at the grocery store when she stocked her kitchen. He had been friendly enough, but she sensed a little distance. She wondered why, but she didn't have the nerve to ask.

She had spent most of her free time this last week with Renae, Rose, and Joe. When she had finally met Joe Rakes, she knew why Renae had fallen for him. It wasn't just his handsome features that made him special. He was a deeply committed Christian whose main objective was to be a good husband and father. He had a gentle spirit and no hangups about his masculinity, so he pitched in with the dishes and the baby like it was second nature to him. Of course, he was conscious of the benefit of his helpfulness. This way, the two of them could have more quality time together each evening. Laura knew these were the characteristics she wanted in the man she hoped to marry.

When the phone rang, Laura was just putting the finishing touches on her makeup. It took extra effort, because she was a little pale after the trying day. She knew she would have to make the evening short if she were to be worth anything on Tuesday. As she took one last look in the mirror, she had to admit that the jade green silk shirtwaist dress did a lot for her coloring. She kept her hair in the same chignon she had worn for school.

"Is this finally Laura?" Gerald's voice sounded slightly irritated. "I've been looking for you. Why didn't you tell me you had moved? I took the room across from you again, I thought, but when I went to pick you up at your door, someone else answered. I was really caught off guard."

Laura could tell this didn't often happen. "I'm sorry. I didn't think about it. Please forgive me."

"All right, Gorgeous. When you ask me in that tone of voice, how can I refuse? How do I get to where you are now?"

"Oh I'm ready, so I'll meet you in the lobby. See you in a minute."

Laura didn't hear his muttered expletive as she hung up the phone. She dashed out the door and took the elevator to the lobby where she was waiting for Gerald when he stepped off the other elevator a few minutes later. Their two weeks apart had not diminished the attraction she felt. If anything, the distance had only enhanced her feelings for him. It was so hard to have complete control over her emotions when she was so tired. She whispered a prayer as she watched him step from the elevator. He was wearing a coffee brown suit with a cream-colored silk shirt. The federal blue tie was flecked with the same colors. The outfit only emphasized his tanned good looks.

He was standing at her elbow. "You seem to be a million miles away."

"I'm sorry. I guess I'm just emotionally drained. You know this was the first day of school, and it was different from anything I could have imagined."

"That's what you get for imagining things," he whispered in her ear. His warm breath disturbed the wispy curls that brushed her cheek. "You should just take things as they come—like I do. That way you aren't often disappointed."

"I guess I've always had a vivid imagination. It's half the fun of things—anticipating."

"I hope you have been anticipating this evening with me. What have you imagined about it?"

"To tell you the truth, I have looked forward to it. However, I was so busy today I didn't have time to imagine anything."

"Too bad. I was going to fulfill your dreams tonight."

"I hate to tell you this, but we'll need to keep the evening pretty short. I'm so tired, and I still have things to do before class starts tomorrow. I can see that the first year of teaching will be the hardest, since I don't have anything to fall back on from other years." Laura didn't see the scowl that clouded Gerald's face for a moment.

"Well, do we have time for dinner?" His voice stung her with its sarcasm. Laura quickly looked into his eyes, but could see nothing but admiration. She must have been mistaken about the change in his tone.

"Of course. I was really disappointed that you had to stay away an extra week."

"I was beginning to wonder. Now, where would you like to go for dinner?"

They decided to try the new restaurant that had opened just outside town on the highway to Fayetteville. Surrounded on three sides by lofty evergreens, the dining room was situated so that it took full advantage of the panoramic view offered by the large picture windows set across the entire front wall.

Since the parking lot was almost full, Gerald let Laura out at the door and went to park the car. As she was waiting in the lobby, Charles and George came out of the dining room. They asked Laura about her first day of school. George seemed especially interested, and she laughingly told him how she had tried in vain to keep ahead of her creative students. Laura had her back to the door, so she didn't see Gerald when he entered. But Charles did. He saw the dark cloud that covered Gerald's face when he saw Laura talking to the two men. By the time he reached them, he had thrown a mask over his emotions.

"Well, I see we've run into a couple of your friends," he said placing his hand possessively in the small of Laura's back.

"Yes." Laura turned to him. "George is interested in

how my first day at school went. I think he feels a little responsible for me since the terrible incident my first week here."

"How thoughtful. Thank you for taking care of Laura for me. It's nice to know I leave her in such competent hands." He was glad to see the questioning look that passed between them. He hoped his remarks had accomplished what he had intended them to. He was staking his claim.

As Laura and Gerald were waiting for their first course to arrive, he regarded her speculatively. "I guess you saw a lot of those two while I was gone."

"Not really." Laura replied without turning her attention from the view. "Charles took me to the lake one day to take my mind off the attack, but that's all the time I spent with either one. Of course, I've seen them at church and around, that's all."

A smile spread across Gerald's face as he announced the arrival of their shrimp cocktails. The dinner proceeded smoothly as they visited. Laura told him about her renewed friendship with Renae. She shared how she had fallen in love with Renae's baby and was very fond of her husband. As she shared the stories of her friendship, Gerald began to relax.

"Sometimes I think my business empire is too big." Gerald interjected.

"What do you mean?"

"I have so many demands on my time and energy. I've been thinking about settling down somewhere and starting a family."

Laura struggled to hide her surprise.

Gerald reached across the table and took Laura's hand in his. "Does that seem so unreasonable?" He sounded amused.

"No...not really...but somehow I didn't think you were the marrying type."

Gerald studied her face for a few minutes before he replied. "I never have thought of myself as the marrying kind either, but sometimes things happen to change our minds. I'm beginning to wonder if you haven't come into my life to change it. You're the first woman who has made me even think about settling down."

Laura looked out the window and tried to absorb what she had heard. She knew she wasn't really ready to settle down with a family just yet, but she also knew that it was definitely what she wanted for her future. She wished she were sure about Gerald's faith in Jesus. She had never heard him say the name of Jesus, even though Gerald had attended church with her more than once.

Gerald began to gently massage the back of her hand with his thumb. "Laura, I don't want to rush you, but I'd like for our relationship to be exclusive. Maybe if we spent more time alone, we could see what the future holds. Would you agree to date only me?"

Laura couldn't see the expression in his eyes. She wished the lighting in the restaurant weren't quite so soft. "Gerald, I'm not dating anyone else right now, but I'm not sure we should make any kind of commitment just yet. I need time to think and pray about it. I will need to pour a lot of energy into this first year of teaching. I've worked so hard to reach this place...but...I don't want to run you off, either." She finished with a whisper and a smile.

"I can accept that, Little Laura." He began to stroke her arm with his other hand. "I won't push you, but you know I want a special place in your life. I'll take you home early tonight, but I want us to spend every evening this week together. I have to be gone next week again." He noticed the thoughtful look on Laura's face. "I'll go to church with you on Wednesday night."

"Okay, but I've started singing in the choir. We practice on Thursday nights."

"How long does that last?"

"Only an hour or so."

"That still leaves time for me." When Gerald smiled, Laura felt herself sink into the depths of his dark eyes. It was as if she were being pulled by a power stronger than her own. His nearness left her almost breathless.

nine

The first week of school went faster than Laura imagined it could. She was beginning to put names with the faces. One stood out from the rest. He was in her tenth grade American History class—Joey Brown. His parents were both dead, and he was living with his grandparents out on War Eagle Creek. His grandparents loved him dearly. So did everyone in Huntington. He was small for his age, but that didn't seem to bother him. He helped his elderly grandparents with their farming. He also worked every odd job he could find. As soon as he was sixteen, he was going to buy himself a car if he had enough money saved.

The blond hair that fell across his forehead almost covered one of his sparkling eyes. He tried to make good grades so he could win a scholarship. He wanted a good education so he could take care of his grandparents. Since he was the son of their youngest child, they were over seventy. They loved him, but they were almost too old to take care of a teenage boy. It would have been too much for them if he had given them any trouble.

Laura had liked the boy since the first day of school. Even the boys who usually would have been considered bullies liked him. Laura had not heard a single person say anything negative about him. He was beginning to have a little trouble with history, so Laura offered to help him after school. She knew how much he wanted to maintain good grades. He didn't want her to do it for nothing, so he came in each day and cleaned her blackboards and emptied her trash. The janitors cleaned the floor every day, but they only emptied the trash twice a week.

On Friday night, Gerald wanted to take Laura somewhere special. They were going to Fort Smith for dinner. There was a place he wanted to show her, but he wouldn't tell her what it was. When they drove under the porte- cochere, Laura wasn't sure she wanted to go in. Instead of a restaurant, it looked like a nightclub to her. Gerald helped her from the car and left it for the valet to park. When they entered the building, a hostess immediately greeted them.

"Mr. Eads, your special reservation is ready," she purred as she led them to a private nook. Laura had glimpsed a bar area to their left as they walked down the hall, but it wasn't near their table.

"Well, Little Laura, how do you like our accommodations?"

"They're fine." Laura was looking at the deep carpet, velvet drapes, and how shielded they were from the other patrons. "The hostess seems to know you. Do you come here often?"

"I've been here on occasion. It's a nice place to take someone when you want them to have a special dinner. I often bring clients here. There are all kinds of things available. If you want to drink, there's a bar." He must have noticed Laura's look of distaste. "I know you don't drink. Some of my clients do drink. You know, when you are in business, you have to deal with all kinds of people."

The evening was special. Laura saw no one else who was in the restaurant except the waitress who was discreet in serving them. Gerald was attentive, but not pushy.

The evening passed quickly. Too soon they were back at the Lodge.

"May I take you to your apartment?" Gerald asked as they stepped into the elevator.

"Yes."

"Little Laura, could I come in for a minute?" Gerald seemed reluctant for the short evening to end.

"Sure. I'll fix us some coffee. . .if you like instant. It's all I have."

"Anything will taste good while I'm with you." Gerald watched her heat the coffee and helped her carry it to the coffee table. After they were seated on the couch, he put his arm around her and pulled her against his shoulder. "I have to leave in the morning, but I'll try to be back in a week. Any time I'm away from you is too long." His lips brushed her hair.

When their coffee was gone, his other hand caressed her cheek before tilting her head back. As he looked into her eyes, Laura saw the fire in his just before his lips touched hers. She closed her eyes as his lips moved across her cheek ever so gently. Then they caressed each closed eyelid before they once again settled on her waiting lips. The kiss began slowly and gently, but grew in intensity.

She responded to the pressure of his lips as her blood rushed through her veins.

Laura had no idea how long the kiss lasted, but it wasn't long enough. She had never been kissed like that before. She wanted it to last forever.

Finally, Gerald pulled away and smiled at the pink flush that colored her face. He stood up and looked down at her. "Little Laura, I love you. I want you to remember that while I'm gone. . .and remember I want us to make a commitment to each other. Are you ready for commitment to me?"

With those words, he opened the door and slipped out. Laura was stunned. After a kiss like that, she had expected him to make other demands. She had been trying to steel herself to turn him down. Maybe he *was* ready for a permanent commitment. She certainly had a lot to ponder that week. Even though she was looking forward to seeing him the next weekend, she would have a hard time falling asleep that night.

The time Laura spent with Joey Brown was productive. He was an intelligent student who was eager to learn. That was refreshing to Laura since she had realized that the majority of her students were just trying to finish school. She was growing to love Joey and had to remind herself to maintain a professional relationship with him. Since he also attended the church where she was a member, she had watched him interact with the other members of the youth group. As he became more and more committed to the

Lord, she saw him developing leadership abilities in that group.

The first week of October, Joey flew into her room after school like a whirlwind with boundless energy. "Miss Bentley, I've got a new job. That means I'll be able to get a car by Christmas. Isn't that wonderful?"

"Oh Joey, that's just great. I'm proud of you. You've been doing so well that you could probably come for tutoring only one day a week."

"That's what I wanted to talk to you about. I really need the other afternoons for my job. Do you think I'm doing that well?"

"Sure. Which afternoon would you like to come?"

"I need to come on Tuesdays if that's all right with you."

"Tuesdays it is then. I'll see you tomorrow. Good luck with the new job."

"Wow, thanks, Miss Bentley," was shouted over his shoulder as Joey rushed out the door and sprinted down the empty hall.

ten

It had been over two weeks since Gerald had left, promising to return in a week and asking her for a commitment. When the week had passed and she hadn't seen him, she expected him at least to call. But, the expected call had never came.

Laura hadn't decided what to do about his question. She certainly wasn't sure that she wanted to be committed to a man who broke promises without an explanation. Then she would remember that last kiss.

The only time she saw Charles was at school and church. He was friendly enough, but slightly aloof. She must have imagined the warm feelings at the lake two weeks before school started, or he had just been especially kind to her because of her attack.

She did see George often because he was in the restaurant each time she had breakfast. They had eaten together several times, and she enjoyed it. It was almost like being with family. The kind of comradery they shared was the same kind she had shared with her brother. . .and she missed him so!

When Laura drove into the driveway of the house in the side of the mountain, she could hear Josie's happy squeal.

Her sunny little face was pressed against the glass of the full-length storm door. What changes one month made in a baby! Tomorrow would be her first birthday, and she was so much more grown-up than the baby Laura had first seen. She loved Laura just as much as Laura loved her. As Laura opened the door, she scooped the blond cherub up and hugged her for a minute until she wriggled to get down.

"Well, hello," Renae called from the kitchen door. "No one gets a welcome like that around here except you and Joe."

"I'm flattered to be accorded such an honor. It's special to me, since I don't have a family of my own anymore. Thanks for sharing yours with me."

"Do I detect wistfulness in that statement, Laura?" Renae was putting the finishing touches on dinner. "When are you going to share what's bothering you? I thought best friends shared everything and helped each other, especially when they are also sisters in Christ."

"What makes you think anything is bothering me?" Laura asked warily.

"Every time we've been together these last two weeks, part of you seems to be somewhere else. I really can't put my finger on it. Just call it woman's intuition."

As Laura gazed into her friend's eyes, she felt her mask begin to slip. "You're right. I need to talk to someone, and I can't think of anyone I would rather confide in."

"As soon as we're through eating, we'll put Josie to bed and then the evening is yours. I'm glad Joe had that meeting tonight. It will give us plenty of time to talk."

Laura's mind did not see the fire her eyes were staring into while Renae put Josie to bed. Earlier, Josie had climbed in her lap and snuggled while Laura rocked her to sleep. Even the talking of the adults in the room didn't disturb her. Little Josie seemed perfectly at peace in Laura's arms. Oh, how those arms ached to hold a child of their own!

"You were a million miles away." Renae's voice interrupted her reverie.

"I was thinking about holding Josie."

Renae went to the kitchen and poured each of them a cup of hot chocolate that had been warming on the stove. "We always could talk better over a cup of hot chocolate," she said, handing a mug to Laura.

"From the size of this mug, you must think we have a lot to talk about."

"Well, don't we?"

When Laura sat and gazed with unseeing eyes at the crackling fire for several minutes, Renae knew it must be really important. She prayed silently for her friend.

"I don't know how to start. I guess I should tell you that since I became a Christian, I haven't dated much. When I first came here, I began to date Gerald Eads. Do you remember the crush I had on him when we were in junior high?"

"How could I forget the tall, dark, handsome bus driver who turned your heart to jello?"

"I never told you about the time he took me up to the lookout on the mountain."

After Laura shared that experience, she told Renae how wary she had been when she had met him as soon as she returned to town. When she told about the dates they had, she described how extravagant Gerald was—and he didn't seem to think anything of it. Although he had attended church with her every time he was in town, Laura wasn't sure he knew Jesus the way they did. Then she told her about how his ardent kisses led to the question of commitment.

"I start to trust him, then he does something like stay away for over two weeks without even calling, and I don't know what to think. Wouldn't you think a man who wanted to be committed to a woman would want to talk to her, even if he couldn't see her?"

"Yes," Renae answered after a thoughtful pause. "I do."

"I know so little about him. Every time I ask him a question about his life, he answers without giving any information. I don't know where he lives. He's told me he owns a restaurant among other business ventures, but I don't know where it is or what the other ventures are."

"How do you know he isn't married or something?"

"When I asked how he had escaped marriage, he gave some flip answer. He told me I'm the first woman who has ever made him want a commitment. Then he disappeared."

"I can see why you're bothered. I thought Mother told me you were dating other men, too."

"Not really. I have had a few dates with Charles Hurd, but they were all before school started. We spent a day at the lake after the attack. It was a wonderful time, and I was beginning to feel drawn to him. He even took me to meet an old mountain woman who is special to him. He has been friendly, but distant, ever since. I don't think he was as interested in me as I thought. I sometimes think I can't trust my emotions. I'm easily swayed."

"What about George Hill? Mother said she's noticed the two of you in the restaurant several times."

"I didn't know she was keeping such close tabs on me," Laura complained in mock exasperation.

"Laura, you know you're important to her. She loves you."

"Oh, I know. And I appreciate her interest. I've been having breakfast with George sometimes. He fills some of the emptiness left by my brother's death."

"I would have never thought of him as being your type."

"Oh? Who is my type?"

"I don't know, but I'm not sure it's Gerald Eads. I have trouble believing that he really knows the Lord. He comes to church with you, but he doesn't seem to be participating.. .He's more like a spectator."

"I guess that's been gnawing at the edge of my consciousness, too. I haven't felt that he was genuinely involving himself in the worship. I've had trouble admitting that to myself. He seems so sincere when he's with me, and I'm drawn by his charisma. I know you can't trust your feelings. I've been able to relax and not be on guard against his advances. I feel safe with him now, though I didn't at first. I admit I was a little suspicious, but being with him has made me relax."

"Laura, you haven't had much experience with men. I did before I became a committed Christian. There are some men who make it their goal in life to prove they can win a Christian woman over to their way of thinking. I've seen some go to great lengths to do it. Is it possible that Gerald could be one of them?"

"I don't think so...Do you have any reason for asking?"

"You know, Laura, men have a sixth sense about men, just like women can see right through a phony woman. Joe hasn't ever wanted you to date Gerald. He senses something about him. I don't know anything specific, but I know he prays a lot for you because of Gerald."

As Laura was getting ready for bed that night, her mind was crowded with all that Renae had said. Where did it fit in with the uneasy feeling she had been having the last several days? She said a special fervent prayer for the Lord to reveal to her in some way what she really needed to know.

At breakfast the next morning, George asked Laura if she would do him a favor. Just as the words were out of his mouth, Charles walked up. "Sit down, Charles. I was just asking Laura if she would help us."

Charles glanced inquiringly at her. "And will she?"

"I haven't told her what we want yet."

"What do you want me to do? You've piqued my curiosity with all this mystery."

"I told you she probably wouldn't want to, anyway," Charles interjected.

"Why don't you let me decide for myself?" Laura sounded disturbed.

"I want you to go on a date with Charles for me."

When Laura's eyes widened with surprise, Charles muttered, "She probably has something else to do."

"I don't know if I have something else to do or not. When is it. . .and why?"

"I need Charles to check something out for me on a case I'm working on. I can't go myself because the people would recognize me. I'd like you to go out to eat with Charles at a club in Fort Smith. You'll need to act like a real dating couple to be convincing."

"I think we could manage that." Laura smiled sweetly. "We have dated a couple of times, you know."

"Are you sure you don't have plans with your tall dark 'friend'?" Charles's tone sounded skeptical.

"I'm sure my social calendar can handle this assignment. When would you like us to go?"

"It needs to be either this weekend or the next," George answered eagerly. "Does this mean you'll do it?"

"Sure. Why not? It sounds like fun." Laura's eyes sparkled with adventure. "Of course, Charles doesn't seem too anxious to spend much time with me." She looked at him accusingly.

"Excuse me," he answered. "I had the impression that your time belonged to someone else. I'm not one to horn in on another man's territory."

"Whatever gave you that idea?" she asked mischievously.

"Who knows?" he answered as he remembered the kisses in the restaurant and the woman stiffening in his embrace in the boat at the lake.

Laura pushed her chair back from the table. "Well, I guess that's all settled then. Just let me know when you need me. I'll be ready," she threw over her shoulder as she hurried to go get ready for school.

Laura and Joyce Ramsey were sitting in the teachers' section of the cafeteria discussing the changes that had come over the students that day.

"I can't explain it. It's as if I have a different group of students from the ones who were in my room yesterday. They all actually want to learn something. Do you think someone switched the real kids with clever imitations?" Laura asked Joyce.

"I remember something like this happening last year, too...just about this time. I think they've just realized that grades come out soon. The ones who were lagging behind are trying to catch up."

"I didn't know it was just a natural phenomenon," Laura exclaimed. "I thought maybe I had done something right."

"What's a natural phenomenon?" Charles slid into the seat across from Laura.

Just as Laura started to answer, Mr. Tounsend called her name over the intercom, asking her to come to the office.

"Looks like you're in trouble now, old girl," Joyce teased as Laura hurriedly disposed of her empty dishes before rushing out the door.

"There you are, Miss Bentley. We have a long distance call for you. You can take it in my office so you can have privacy. It's on line two."

"Thank you, Mr. Tounsend."

As Laura closed the door, she was apprehensive. She hoped nothing had happened to her grandparents.

"Hello, Little Laura." The familiar voice inspired a picture of dark curls and deep brown eyes, and Laura couldn't help smiling to herself.

"Gerald, is it really you?" Laura stammered as a thrill rushed down her spine.

"Of course ,it's me."

"Where have you been?" Laura blurted out without thinking.

"Have you missed me then?" The deep chuckle reached to Laura's heart. "I've been tied up with some important business. Have you been considering our last conversation?"

"Yes, I have, and I think the two of us need to have a long talk as soon as possible."

"How about tomorrow night, Little Laura?"

"Tomorrow is Wednesday night. Will you go to church with me? I'll be helping lead the music in worship."

"Of course, Sweetie. I wouldn't miss it for the world. I can pick you up just before church time."

"Well, I'm afraid that won't work because I have to be at the church early. Those of us who are going to be involved in the service will have a prayer time before the service starts."

"You will be eating sometime, won't you?"

"Yes, I plan to eat after the service. I sing much better if I haven't just eaten."

"Okay. Little Laura, I'll meet you at the church. Do you think you can get a ride there with someone? I want you to ride with me after the service."

"Sure. George Hill also has a part in the service. I'm sure he won't mind taking me. Oh, the bell just rang. I have to go now. I'll look forward to tomorrow night."

As Laura left the office, she met Joyce in the hall.

"You don't look like you were in too much trouble judging by the smile on your face and the glow in your eyes."

"No. I had a long distance phone call, and it has given me a new outlook on tomorrow."

eleven

Laura had dressed with special care for the service. She had chosen a plaid shirtwaist dress. The flared skirt draped softly just below her shapely knees. She wore her hair in a simple French braid which extended below the neck of her dress. She smiled wistfully as she added her mother's pearl choker and earrings.

On the way to church, George told Laura about the plans for the date with Charles. When they went to the nightclub, everyone who saw them would need to believe they were really dating. They had to wait until the next weekend and go either on Friday or Saturday night. He would let her know later which one. As he stopped the car in the parking lot of the church, he turned to her and covered her small hand with his big one.

"I can't tell you, Laura, how much this means to me. It's very important to my investigation. I don't think there'll be any danger, or I wouldn't let you go. You're becoming very important to me, you know—like the sister I never had. I hope you feel the same way."

"I do. You've filled some of the emptiness that was left when I lost my brother."

As Laura looked past George, she saw Charles standing in the door of the church looking in their direction. She smiled at him as George got out and came around to open the door for her. He must not have seen her, because he turned and entered the building without a greeting.

After the prayer time, the singles group that was leading the service went into the sanctuary and was seated on the platform. When Laura scanned the crowd for the dark, curly head and couldn't find it, she concentrated on the service. It was the first time she had had the opportunity to sing a solo since she had joined the church, and she was a little apprehensive. Concentrating on the service wasn't hard for her because she loved to be in the Lord's house and felt so blessed that He saw fit to use whatever talent she had. When she got up to sing, it was for Him. Her clear, sweet tones filled the room until many eyes were brimming with tears. She sang with emotion which sprang from her own unique experience with the Lord. As she sat down, her prayer was one of humble thanks for having been able to serve.

The music helped prepare everyone's hearts for the testimony and sharing time that the others in the singles group had planned. Many of the people in the congregation were touched by the obvious presence of God that night.

The service was ending before Laura thought to look for Gerald again. She still didn't see him in the crowd and was beginning to wonder if he had stood her up. She was starting out the door of the sanctuary when he entered from the outside door. Her heart did a little flip when he looked straight into her eyes and smiled.

"Are you ready to eat? I've made reservations at the restaurant at the lookout. We need to hurry if we're going to be there in time."

"How did you like the service?" Laura asked when they were seated in the car.

"I was held up at a meeting, so I just got there when you came from the sanctuary...I'm sorry I missed hearing you sing. Would you sing just for me sometime?"

"Sure...sometime."

When they reached the restaurant, they were escorted to a table next to the window. Laura looked out and drank in the scenery. She didn't notice that Gerald was ordering until he was almost finished. When she turned to look at him, the waitress had a dreamy look in her eyes as she watched Gerald. Laura wondered if she would ever get used to that. She should be proud to be seen with a man whom other women admired. Of course, he never flirted with any of them while he was with her.

"Now we can talk until our order is ready, Little Laura. Have you missed me?"

"Of course I have."

"Does that mean I'm becoming important in your life?"

"I think so...Gerald...you are important to me."

"How important? Important enough for you to make that commitment we talked about?"

"Gerald, when I make a commitment to a man, it will be a once-in-a-lifetime commitment."

Gerald reached across the table and took her hands in his. The warmth from his hands seemed to spread to her very heart.

"Laura, what's standing in the way? I want you, and I need you. I don't think I've ever needed a woman in this way before. I'm not speaking of a physical relationship now. I need you to make me a whole man. You give me balance, Laura."

"Gerald, this is hard for me to say. . .I don't know how to start. . .but, I can never be married to a man who is not a Christian. And I'm not sure in my heart that you are."

"I know I don't seem to be quite as strong a Christian as you are. I'll try to do better for you, if it's important to you."

"You don't understand at all. I can only marry a man who is completely committed to Jesus. It won't work if he only becomes a Christian for me. There's a big difference."

"Little Laura, can we continue as we have been and let me try to learn what you're talking about?"

Laura glanced down at their hands as he gave her an encouraging squeeze. "Yes. . .I like the way our relationship is now. . .I'll pray for the Lord to send someone to you who can teach you what I mean."

Gerald looked past Laura's shoulder, welcoming the interruption. "Here's dinner. Let's enjoy the view and the time we have together."

When Gerald left Laura at her apartment, he told her he would be back on Saturday night. "Will you save it for me?"

Laura agreed. How could she deny him that?

When Laura was in the school cafeteria on Friday, Charles slid into the chair across from her. "Where's Joyce? I thought you two usually had lunch together."

"She has a parent-teacher conference she's preparing for. I'm glad you have this lunch period, too. I don't like to eat alone."

"Neither do I. So how's your first year of teaching so far?"

Laura began to tell Charles what she liked about teaching. Then she shared a few things she didn't like as well, but she ended on a positive note.

"I'm glad to see you take so much interest in the activities at the church. I was blessed by the service Wednesday night," Charles offered enthusiastically.

"I was, too. Jesus was so real to me that night."

"It's too bad your friend didn't come in for the service. He might have been blessed, too."

"What do you mean?"

"I was outside the sanctuary doors when he drove up. You couldn't miss that silver Cadillac. I kept expecting him to come in, but he didn't until the service was over. He got out of his car when the doors to the sanctuary first opened after the service. Too bad he didn't come in. He should have heard you sing. If anything could have moved him, that would have."

Laura sat stunned as the bell rang. It "didn't compute", as the students would say. Gerald had said he had been held up in a meeting and had just arrived when she saw him. Now Charles said he had been sitting in the car all the time. Did Charles know what he was talking about? Of course, he had no way of knowing what Gerald had told her. He was just passing the time of day with her. Just then, she remembered she had asked the Lord to show her what she needed to know. Was this something He had wanted her to find out about Gerald? Maybe Gerald would have a logical explanation on Saturday night.

Laura was glad Joe and Renae had asked her to spend the evening with them. She didn't want to be alone, and since she had shared her dilemma with Renae, she wanted Joe's input as well. Since Renae didn't keep secrets from him, he would know about their earlier discussion. She needed some feedback from him.

As she drove into the driveway, she saw the pixie face pressed against the glass. How would it feel to have a beautiful baby and a Godly man for a husband? She hoped she would soon find out, but who did she know that would fill that bill? George Hill would, but not for her. Since he was like a brother, she knew she could never feel romantic about him. Of course, there was Charles Hurd. She had felt an attraction for him earlier, but he had only been helping her over a hurt. He couldn't feel anything special for her. He was just a brother in the Lord, but he was a Godly man who would make someone a wonderful husband.

As she scooped up the little blond and snuggled her, raining kisses around the soft neck, Josie laughed and squealed with delight. Laura sniffed her sweet baby scent and felt the velvety softness of her skin.

"Since Joe's already home, I knew it had to be you, Laura," Renae shouted from the kitchen.

After the meal, Laura sat by the fire in the den while Joe and Renae put Josie to bed. She looked up as Joe entered the room.

"I think we need a couple more logs. I'll get them." He went through the door to the patio.

"Did you get that little bundle of energy to finally settle down?"

"Renae is rocking her in her own room after her bath. We think she'll settle down better there. She was really wound up." Joe stirred the fire and put the other wood on it. "It's good for her to have other adults she loves. . .You seem to have something on your mind. We thought you needed more adult company tonight."

"How astute you are. I didn't know it showed so much. Did Renae share with you what she and I talked about earlier this week?"

"Yes, do you mind?"

"Oh, no. I was hoping the three of us might get a chance to talk about it."

"Talk about what?" Renae entered from the bedroom wing. ". . .Or do I already know?"

"Am I so transparent? Both you and Joe could sense I wanted to discuss Gerald. He called me Tuesday at school. . .long distance, at noon. He apologized for not getting in touch with me during the time he was gone. He told me he had been tied up with business, and he would come

Wednesday night to see me. He would even go to church with me."

"Oh, I didn't see him in church. I'm glad he got to hear you sing," Renae interjected.

"He didn't hear me sing. He wasn't there, or at least he didn't come in. He came to the door as I was leaving the sanctuary. He told me he had been held up at a business meeting, but Charles told me in passing at lunch today that Gerald was there all the time, sitting in his car on the parking lot. Afterward we went to the lookout restaurant and had a serious discussion about commitment. I told him I couldn't marry a man who didn't know Jesus like I do. He wanted us to continue dating, and he would try to learn about Jesus. Of course, I didn't know then that he had been outside the church all evening. That puts a different light on our discussion. You don't think Charles could have lied to me, do you?"

"What reason could he have?" Joe queried.

"I've been asking myself the same thing. I had prayed the Lord would let me find out anything I should know about Gerald. Do you think that might be why Charles told me this? Could God have prompted him to share it without his even knowing it?"

"I think you know the answer to that, Laura," Renae said gently. "It's hard sometimes to accept what the Lord is trying to tell us."

"Gerald promised he would come Saturday night. I don't know how to bring this up, or what to say to him. I also don't know what to do about me."

"What do you mean, Laura?" Joe asked tenderly.

"I don't know if I'll ever be able to trust my emotions. I was falling for Gerald. I wanted to believe him when he told me something. My desire was for something to develop between us. You see, I'm ready to settle down and have a family, and he is the only man who's interested. I'm so confused."

"Let's covenant together right now to pray about this problem in Laura's life. We need to pray for a definite, unquestionable word from the Lord to you, Laura." Joe took Renae's and Laura's hands. The two young women closed the circle as they bowed their heads.

twelve

As Laura luxuriated in a bubble bath on Friday evening preparing for her date with Charles, she thought back over the past week. It had been a difficult week both emotionally and physically. She had been working on mid-term grades. This first time it hurt to have to give failing grades to any of her students. She felt like she had somehow failed them. Joyce had said she had felt the same way, but that it was just part of being a teacher. Laura had spent time going over all her lesson plans to see if maybe she hadn't been specific enough—or helpful enough. She had wanted to be a teacher for a long time, but she had never thought about the possibility of students failing her classes. It really was going to take some getting used to. Maybe next time it would be easier.

That week had been hard for other reasons, too. Gerald had not shown up on Saturday night. She had waited and worried about how to bring up the problem she was having with their relationship. He hadn't come, and he hadn't called either. She was disappointed, but in a way, she was also relieved that she hadn't had to deal with it. Now she wished they had been able to discuss it. The worrying was worse than any discussion could ever have been. Also, if they had discussed it, she wouldn't be feeling so unsettled.

George had eaten breakfast with her a couple of times that week. She always had fun when she was with him. He had begun to tell her about a girl he was interested in. He said he had trouble sharing about his deep feelings even with his best friend, Charles, and he wanted to talk to her to get a woman's point of view. She was honored that he could trust her with something that important. She would keep his secret.

She took from her closet the only after-five dress she owned. It was a rich turquoise blue—her favorite color because it enhanced her eyes. The chiffon softly draped into a V at the neck and the hem swirled around her knees. She always wore a gold belt with it, because her one pair of dressy sandals was gold with rhinestone clasps on the toes. Her grandmother's favorite costume jewelry completed her accessories. She wore her hair braided again, but wound it around her head like a coronet. She looked critically at her image in the mirror. Charles would have no reason to be ashamed to be seen with her.

When she opened the door to her suite, Charles let out a slow whistle. He definitely did not appear to be the least bit ashamed.

"Why, Miss Bentley, you've never looked like this at school or church. You've been holding out on us?" he teased.

"You don't look like that at school or church either," she teased back. And it was true. He was wearing a black tuxedo with satin lapels and a satin stripe down the sides of the trousers. The red studs and red cummerbund set off the white pleated shirt and black tie. "I'll be proud to be seen with you."

"I had no idea what you were wearing, but I think this will look just right with that dress." He pulled a florist's corsage box from behind his back. Nestled in green tissue paper was a huge white orchid adorned with a cluster of gold ribbon.

"Charles, I didn't know you were going to get me a corsage. Thank you, but I wish I had known. I would have gotten you a boutonniere."

"Never fear, George took care of that when he bought this flower. The investigation is underwriting us tonight. I thought you knew that."

"I guess I just didn't think. Neither one of you told me."

"Laura, George said to tell you we are to treat this like a special celebration, so anything on the menu goes. None of that 'waiting until your date orders to see what he can afford'. We have relatively unlimited funds."

"Well, isn't that nice?" Laura said as Charles helped her into her coat. "Too bad it isn't for real."

"You're right, too bad," Charles muttered under his breath as he turned and locked her door behind them.

The ride to Fort Smith was breathtaking in the crisp autumn air. The stars looked close enough to touch, and the bright moon cast a pearly coating over the autumn leaves, muting their rich colors. It seemed an unseen artist had shaken his brush over the landscape, casting splotches of color along the mountainsides.

"I just love fall in the Ozarks," Laura whispered. "I've

never seen so many brilliant colors anywhere else. Every variation of every color you can imagine. Even the browns are vibrant. None of those drab autumn leaves like I've seen other places."

"I know what you mean. Each season feels like my favorite while it's happening, but I may be a little partial to fall. I like to tramp the woods in the fall. Have you ever done that?"

"Not really. During the fall, I was in school, and Dad didn't take me with him."

"Say, how about going with me this weekend? I'll show you what it's like. Granny has been asking when I'd bring you back to see her. This time we could get there by climbing over the mountain instead of going across the lake. What do you say?"

Laura turned to look at him before she gave her answer. She took so long to answer that Charles glanced toward her. He must have liked what he saw, because a smile curved his lips as he turned back to the road.

"You know I can't look at you very much and get us to Fort Smith safely. These roads are dangerous enough in the daytime. With small animals roaming the mountains at night, I can't take a chance of not seeing something in the road."

"I'm sorry, Charles. I'd love to go 'tramping' over the mountain to Granny's with you. Should we go tomorrow or Sunday afternoon?"

"Why don't we decide on the way home tonight? We don't know for sure how late we'll be."

"Okay." Laura snuggled down in the seat. Charles reached over and put his arm around her. He gently pulled her closer without taking his eyes off the road.

"Is this where we're going?" Laura asked as Charles turned off the street into the driveway in front of the club.

"Yes. . .Why?"

"I've been here before."

"When?"

"Gerald brought me here some time last month." Laura felt Charles stiffen and then relax.

"Did he take you into the club?"

"No. He had made special arrangements so that we stayed in the dining area."

Laura couldn't see the scowl on Charles's face as he went around to open the car door for her. He helped her out and handed his keys to the parking valet. Gently putting his arm around her, he guided her to the entrance of the club. A statuesque blond in a very revealing uniform escorted them to their seats at a table near the dance floor. Laura couldn't help feeling the girl looked familiar, but she was sure she hadn't seen her when she was there with Gerald.

As they were seated, Charles looked around to see the layout. He was pleased they could see not only the dance floor and stage, but also into the bar.

"I know you don't feel too comfortable in a place like this," he said, ". . .but it's important that I see as much as possible. George couldn't come and do this, because they might suspect an investigation if he were here."

Laura reached across the table and lightly brushed his arm with her fingertips. "I agreed to come knowing it would be a place like this. It appealed to my sense of adventure. Right now I need something like this in my life. It sounded like fun, and I'll be helping George. I'm glad to do that."

Charles studied Laura as she was taking in the surroundings. She thought the room was much too dark. Of course, there were candles on each table, but they were for effect, not for the light they gave. The wallpaper and carpet looked expensive, as well as the heavy draperies that hung everywhere. Laura didn't like them, though. She preferred light and color, and everything here was dark and gloomy. The spacious room was a honeycomb of private nooks and niches, with the thick drapes and many large plants serving as screens.

"When I was looking around the room, I thought about the scriptures that talk about darkness and light. I do like for a place to have atmosphere, but a place like this makes me think about people who have something to hide." Laura turned to Charles. "Does it make you feel that way, too?"

"I guess I hadn't thought about it that way, but you're right. We'd better go ahead and decide what to order before the waitress comes. Did you have anything special in mind? We can go all out."

"Why don't you order for me? There isn't anything on the menu I don't like," Laura answered as the waitress approached the table.

"Could I get you anything from the bar while you're deciding?" she asked sweetly.

"No," Charles quickly answered. "I think we're ready to order dinner."

"Certainly, sir."

As Charles ordered, Laura continued to study the room. She also looked at the waitress, trying not to stare. The waitress was dressed in an even skimpier costume than the hostess. Her black silky skirt was so short that about the only thing covering her legs were her mesh hose. Her blouse was a peasant style, which bared her shoulders. When she reached for the menus, Laura wondered how she kept the blouse from falling off. Laura glanced at Charles when the girl was picking up the menus. She was surprised and pleased that he was smiling at her instead of the voluptuous waitress. He leaned forward and took her hand.

"I hope you'll relax and enjoy the evening with me."

Her smile answered for her. The soft music coming from the band on stage added to the romantic mood of the place. She liked the way his hand sheltered hers. She was going to enjoy playing the part of a girl in love with her escort. It wouldn't be hard, because Charles was the kind of man she would like for a husband. It was too bad he wasn't interested in her. When he slid around the booth until he was close to her, she was glad. They were sitting side by side with his arm around her waist.

"I guess this is why they have circular tables—it's more

intimate," she murmured.

"No complaints here," he grinned.

Charles had ordered prime rib for both of them, and it had been the best Laura had ever eaten. The whole evening was turning out to be better than she had anticipated. The time with Charles was informative, too. He shared more of his life with her than he had before, and her respect for him grew. When he finally told her he had to check on a few things, she took the time to go to the ladies' room and freshen up.

Instead of a restroom, it was a lounge as posh as the rest of the club. The main room had soft pink walls and plush red carpet. White velvet chaise lounges and occasional chairs were scattered around the large room. Each chair and chaise had a small, brass-and-glass table beside it. All the lamps in the room were also brass with white shades. It looked like a sitting room, or an old-fashioned "withdrawing" room. An arch at the end of one wall led to an alcove with a lighted mirror for makeup repairs. Beyond this, the facilities were private and luxurious.

Laura had never been in such a ladies' lounge. It made her want to relax on one of the chaises. However, she sat on the plush, white, cushioned brass stool in front of the mirror and surveyed her face to see what, if any, improvements could be made.

As she applied her lipstick, her neck prickled as if someone were watching her. Her attention shifted to the reflection of the archway in the mirror. Sure enough, the hostess who had seated them was leaning against the wall with her arms folded across her chest. Laura didn't try to conceal the question in her eyes.

"I see you've found someone to date besides a married man," the blond said.

For a moment Laura could only stare at her, dumbfounded, before she asked, "What are you talking about?"

"The last two times I saw you, you were with a married man."

"I think you have me confused with someone else," Laura stammered. The woman had to be confused, yet something about her did look strangely familiar.

"No, I'm not confused. I made sure I got a good look at you the last time I saw you. I wanted to remember exactly what you looked like."

A scene flashed into Laura's mind of a blond-haired woman looking her over from head to toe before she shut the door at another ladies' room. So that was why the woman looked familiar. She had seen her before, but she looked different. Laura remembered a smartly dressed woman with tasteful makeup. This woman looked like a woman of the street with her excessive makeup and inappropriate costume.

"Now I remember seeing you before. . .but why would you want to remember what I look like?"

The other woman stood away from the wall and took a step toward Laura. "Because it was my husband you were with! I knew he would eventually bring you here. He always parades his 'friends' in front of me, but he brought you on my day off." Sarcastic sweetness burned through her voice, and her eyes glittered with malice. "Gerald and I are separated, but he has never asked me for a divorce. Sometimes, he even comes home to me for a week or two, and we try to make our marriage work again."

Laura couldn't help wondering if that was where Gerald had been when he hadn't called for so long.

As if in answer to her question, the woman continued, "We were together a couple of weeks in September. He has strayed off and on throughout our marriage. I can always tell when he's found another interest. When I find out, I try to get a look at her. He's especially drawn to pure types like you. I guess it gives him a change from his usual fare. You certainly seem a cut above his past selections, though. Somehow you look a little different." Her tone had changed somewhat, and her voice trailed off, as if she were in thought.

Laura's eyes were glazed with pain, but the other woman continued as if the words were a flood and she was powerless to stem the flow. "He asked me to come back to work in the club when his hostess had to take a medical leave of absence. Of course, that was over a year ago. I'm surprised you would come to Gerald's club with your new love."

Laura felt like a dagger had been driven through her mid-section.

"Don't take it so hard, Dearie. I didn't know you had fallen so hard. I didn't realize he had spent that much time with you. I've tried to keep him busy and interested until this thing blew over." With this announcement, Gerald's wife looked at herself in the mirror, adjusted the neckline of her costume, and sauntered out the door. Laura could scarcely catch her breath as tears slowly overflowed.

Another scene pushed its way into her consciousness— Joe and Renae holding her hands and praying for her to discover what she needed to know about Gerald. This was the answer to that prayer, but how could she face the next few minutes. . .or hours. . .or days. . .or weeks? She laid her head on her folded arms. Her body shook with the force of her sobs. How could she have been such a fool?

Laura didn't know how long she had sat there when she heard the outer door to the ladies' lounge open. She sat up and dried her tears. As she looked at the streaks they had left on her face, she took out her compact and powdered her cheeks. It didn't do any good, so she got a towel and moistened it with cold water. After placing it over her eyes for a few minutes, the discoloration and puffiness improved. Then she applied a heavy layer of powder. This camouflaged the damage enough that she was able to look at the two women who were in the lounge without hiding her face. She hurried toward the door.

As Laura started down the hall, she saw a couple wrapped in an intimate embrace in the shadows of the hallway. "That's all I need," she thought as she stopped. Just then they parted, and the man glanced into her eyes. She recognized the deep brown pools. Gerald looked at her for a moment before recognition lit his eyes, followed by a quick realization of what was happening. He was holding his wife in a loving embrace, while the woman to whom he had lied about his marital status was coming down the hall toward them. Laura saw all of this before Gerald was able to cover his tracks. He quickly pushed the other woman toward the dining room, but she wouldn't be pushed far. He continued to watch Laura as she looked in the other direction and tried to go past them.

"Aren't you even going to speak to me?" He reached for her arm.

She pulled her arm from his grasp and turned blazing eyes on him. "Were you speaking to me?" Her voice was like ice.

"Little Laura, what's wrong?" he asked smoothly. How could Laura have ever liked the sound of his voice? Now it sounded harsh and grated on her tattered nerves.

"I've just met your wife." How could she be speaking coherently when her thoughts were so jumbled?

Just then some new patrons entered the club, and the blond went to greet them. "Surely she told you we're separated. I'm going to get a divorce so we can be married, Laura." This lie didn't sound nearly as convincing as his others had.

"How could you think I would marry you? I won't break up a marriage, and I won't marry a man who is involved in this type of...business." Laura gestured toward the bar.

"Who are you to point a finger? Aren't you here using this 'business'?...Haven't you been here before?...Didn't you enjoy the things this 'business' paid for? All you goody-two-shoes are alike."

How could Laura have ever thought he was handsome? The sneer on his face transformed him into someone she could never have loved. The signs of dissipation showed clearly now. Laura stood there as if paralyzed. She couldn't move one muscle, because she was in shock.

"You girls are all so gullible. You knew what I was like, yet you took the chance that I had changed. You believed what you wanted to. I never told you I wasn't married. You asked me why I wasn't. I only answered your question. Not all married men wear a ring on their left hand. That's what all you innocents look for." Gerald chuckled. "It almost worked this time, didn't it?"

"No!" Laura screamed as she covered her ears with her hands. She swayed as if she were going to faint, but two strong arms encircled her from behind.

"Well, if it isn't the white knight in the black tuxedo," Gerald sneered. "You're one of the reasons I sought Little Laura as my own. I saw the way you looked at her the first night she came to Huntington. You wanted her as much as I did. I saw the desire in your eyes as you watched her walk to the Lodge. I wanted to show you and your pal, George, what a real man does when he desires a woman."

Charles had a hard time controlling his rage.

"Well, she's all yours now," Gerald threw over his shoulder as he entered his private office and slammed the door.

Charles stood in the dark hall and held Laura. He had to fight his thoughts about the monster who had just left them. Gerald could never understand the difference between the way the two men desired her. Until that very moment, Charles had not admitted to himself that he wanted more than anything to marry Laura. It had been an unnamed longing since that first night.

Charles hoped that Laura hadn't been aware of what Gerald had said. He knew how devastated she would be if she had. She was still trembling with her head buried against his chest. He held her close until she calmed, all the time praying that the Lord would minister to the bruised and bleeding emotions of the girl in his arms.

When Laura quit shaking, he took her to the table. Then he paid the bill and made arrangements for the car to be brought to the door. On his return, she was just sitting and staring. He knew she was suffering from shock. He gently helped her into the car and, after he closed his door, tenderly drew her toward him, pulling her head to his shoulder. As he wheeled out of the parking lot, he held her to him. When they were on the highway, he continued to hold her as he surrounded her with whispered prayers and promises.

Laura hadn't stirred from the shelter of his arms since they had left Fort Smith. Charles didn't want to take her to her suite to be alone, so he turned around in the lot of the Lodge and drove to the house in the side of the mountain, praying all the way that a light would be on. He didn't want to wake them up if they had already gone to bed. He breathed a prayer of thanks as he turned into the driveway and saw a warm glow from the kitchen window. He didn't want to leave Laura in the car by herself, so he sounded the horn gently, hoping Joe or Renae would hear. Joe came to investigate. He rushed out when he recognized the car and helped Charles take Laura in the house. Renae held the door open for the men.

"What happened to Laura?" Renae was frantic. "Is she hurt?"

"Only emotionally." Charles helped Laura to the couch. "She's had a terrible shock tonight. I didn't think I should leave her at her place alone. I took a chance at least one of you would be up. I know how much the two of you love her."

You, too, Renae thought, but she didn't say it. She could see how haggard Charles looked—as if he, himself, had sustained the shock. She went to the kitchen to fix some hot tea. Laura probably needed it. When she returned, Charles was sitting on the couch holding Laura. Joe was grimly staring into the fire as he leaned on the mantel.

"Is anyone going to tell me what happened?"

thirteen

When Laura awoke on Saturday morning, she felt the pain deep inside. She couldn't remember why it was there, but it was so strong. When she finally opened her eyes, she wondered where she was. Nothing looked familiar. She was in a bedroom, but it wasn't her own. She looked down at the nightgown she was wearing, and it wasn't hers, either. Was she still dreaming? She couldn't remember what they were, but she had had terrible nightmares. Maybe that was why she hurt, but that wouldn't explain the bedroom and nightgown. Sitting up in bed and looking around, she was surprised to see someone asleep in a chair at the foot of the bed. The drapes were drawn, so the room was shadowed. Who could it be? She was just thinking about looking for help when Renae returned to the room.

"So you finally woke up?" questioned a cheery voice as Renae went to the window and opened the drapes. The sun streaming in the window told Laura it wasn't very early in the morning. "I was beginning to think you weren't ever going to wake up."

"Renae, I'm sorry. . .but I don't know where I am or why I'm here," Laura's voice was quiet. "Has something happened. . . and who is in that chair?"

As if in answer to her question, Charles stirred, sat up,

and stretched.

"What's going on? Why am I here, and why is he in this bedroom with me?" Laura was becoming hysterical.

Renae rushed to the bed and put her arms around Laura. "Everything's okay. Don't panic. You had a shock last night. Charles didn't want to leave you alone. He took the liberty of bringing you to our house. You're in our guest room. I dressed you in my nightgown and put you to bed, but Charles wanted to sit with you in case you needed someone during the night. Joe and I have been here much of the night, too."

Laura turned and looked at Charles who was now standing. What she saw reached her soul. He came to the side of the bed and took her hands in his, wearing his heart in his eyes.

"I think I'll go home and get some rest. I'm leaving you in good hands. I'll be back later this afternoon, and we'll discuss our date to tramp the woods." He raised her fingers to his mouth and gently touched them with his lips. He released them and was out the door before Laura could reply.

Laura had breakfast with Renae and Joe. Their gentle, probing questions eased her into talking about what had happened in Fort Smith. It hadn't been easy, but finally Laura had been able to share all she could remember. Then she told them how the scene of the three of them praying had come to her when she found out that Gerald was married. She talked and cried, then talked and cried some more.

"I feel like such a fool," she sobbed. "I feel unworthy of the Lord's love. I was willfully dating a married man."

"Now Laura," Joe said gently. "You didn't actually know. Women who haven't had much experience with men aren't prepared to deal with someone like Gerald Eads. You're not to blame."

"How can you say that? There must have been something about me that attracted him."

"Laura, it was your purity. Some men see purity as a challenge. The fault was in Gerald, not you."

"I don't know if I can ever trust my emotions again. I wanted a husband and family. I let that desire blind me to any faults he might have."

"Laura, this will pass, and maybe you'll be better for it."

Laura had just finished dressing in her jeans and a jade green sweatshirt when the phone rang. For a minute, she didn't want to answer it. She didn't want to talk to anyone, and there was always the possibility it might be Gerald trying to get in touch with her. She hadn't been totally aware of what the two men had said to each other in the hall of the club. She let it ring several times before she decided she should answer it. It might be Joe and Renae, and they would worry if she didn't answer.

"I was just about to hang up and come check on you when you finally answered." A worried masculine voice answered her timid, "Hello."

"Charles, I'm sorry. I didn't want to talk to anyone. Then I decided if you or Joe and Renae called, you would worry if I didn't answer the phone."

"You're right. I thought you were going to stay at Joe and Renae's until I called. I called there and found you'd gone."

"I didn't have anything to wear except the dress from last night. I wanted to come home and get into something comfortable."

"How are you planning to spend the rest of your day?"

"I guess I hadn't really thought. I just wanted to come home and change clothes."

"Well, think about it." Charles's voice was gentle. "We had talked about hiking across the mountain today or tomorrow. Let me come get you. Being in the beauty of nature should be relaxing for you."

Laura took a minute to consider that. She looked around the suite. There was nothing there but memories. "I believe you're right. I don't want to be alone all day. I'll be ready in half an hour. What do I need to bring?"

"Only your beautiful self. I'll take care of everything else. I'll be there as soon as I can."

Laura put on some old walking shoes, then looked around for something to take to Granny Thrush. She was looking forward to seeing the older woman again. Laura hoped they would have a few minutes to talk alone. Just then she spotted a paperweight she had made in school before her family had been killed. It held a picture of her whole family. She picked it up and stuck it in the backpack she was taking to carry a few essentials. Also, if she found some rocks or leaves she could use to decorate her room at school, she could carry them and keep her hands free.

It was about forty minutes before she heard the firm knock on her door. She had begun to worry that something had happened. She threw the door open wide. When she did, the first thing she saw were those intense blue eyes. She had not realized before how really blue they were because she had been blinded by brown ones.

"I'm sorry I took so long. I went to the store to pick up a few things. The lines are long on Saturday. I hurried as fast as I could."

"That's all right, Charles. I'm ready to go. Just let me get my backpack. Will I need a coat?"

"It's not very cold now, but you might need a jacket later. I could carry it in my backpack if you want me to."

"I'm taking my backpack. I'll put it in there. Is it very windy?"

"Not really, why?"

"I guess I'll leave my hair loose if it isn't windy. I'll put a scarf in my backpack just in case I need it later." Laura didn't see the expression on Charles's face, because she was putting the scarf in the backpack. He was watching her red hair ripple as it fell around her shoulders. For a second, he started to reach for it, but then pulled his hand back.

"Are we ready now?" he asked as he opened the door for her.

The ride out of town was a pleasant one. They talked about Future Teachers, the weather, and how beautiful the leaves looked. This small talk began to work as a healing balm to Laura's bruised emotions. She was glad she wasn't sitting at home feeling sorry for herself.

"Thank you for asking me to go with you. I don't think I should have stayed home today. I appreciate your thoughtfulness." She looked out over the mountains. She couldn't quite bring herself to look at him when she said it.

Laura didn't see any kind of road where Charles turned off the highway. It just seemed to be a break in the trees and underbrush.

"Won't it hurt your car to drive it here?"

"No. I've driven here before. We aren't going far. We'll leave the car in a clearing up ahead." Just then they topped a rise in the ground and entered a clearing that looked like a meadow.

"What a beautiful spot!" Laura couldn't help exclaiming. "I'd bet this place is beautiful no matter what the season."

"And you'd be right," Charles agreed heartily. "This is one of my favorite places in the mountains. I've spent many happy hours here. We'll leave the car at the far end of the clearing, then climb over the mountain to Granny's cabin. Are you sure you're up to that? It might be strenuous."

"Strenuous exercise is just what I need. You'll let me stop and rest sometimes, won't you?"

"Of course." Charles didn't realize how tender his voice sounded. Laura turned to look at him curiously, but he was watching where he was trying to park the car in the shade.

Charles led her between two trees to a path she didn't see until they were on it. It led through an area that looked like a specially planted arbor. The limbs wove in and out of each other as they arched above the path, creating speckled shadows on the fallen leaves under their feet. It was so beautiful. Laura began to kick the leaves as she walked.

"My mother never let me kick leaves. She didn't want me to ruin my shoes. I'm glad I wore my old ones." Laura began to skip and kick the leaves every two or three steps.

Charles watched her for a minute, then ran after her. His heartbeat accelerated as he watched her running with her long red hair dancing behind her. When he caught up with her, he threw his arms around her and pulled her close to his chest. Her hair fell around her shoulders like a veil. Her eyes widened in surprise and anticipation.

Laura realized what he was going to do as his lips tenderly caressed hers. The feather light touch quickly became more intense. Laura responded for a heartbeat before she stiffened in his arms.

"I'm sorry." Charles recognized the panic in Laura's eyes as their lips drew apart. "I didn't plan to do that. I know you're vulnerable right now, and I would never do anything to hurt you." He continued to hold her loosely in his arms. "Please forgive me for being insensitive."

Laura leaned her head against his broad chest. "I didn't mean to react that way. I know you are a different kind of man than. . .he is." She couldn't bring herself to speak his name on this special afternoon.

Charles kept one arm around Laura as they started up the

path again. They walked this way for a few minutes, each one lost in his own thoughts. The overhanging trees made a corridor as they made progress along the path. Soon they came to the end of it. To Laura it looked like they had come up against a wall, because there was a large boulder blocking their way.

Charles took her hand and led her around one end of the rock formation. "It might not be easy to climb up this path, but I know you can do it." He stepped ahead, guiding her.

By the time they were halfway up the side of the mountain, Laura was ready to agree it wasn't an easy climb, but she didn't complain. The physical exertion was good for her. Her body came alive with the exercise and the good clean air. She enjoyed looking at the different kinds of plants they saw.

Many times she had to ask Charles what something was. They reached a shelf of rock about two-thirds of the way up the mountain.

"I think it's time for a break." Charles removed his backpack.

Part of the shelf of rock made a low seat, where Laura took off her backpack and sat down. It felt good to be leaning against something.

"Isn't it thoughtful of God to provide such a marvelous bench for tired climbers?" She looked at Charles. "What are you doing?"

Charles was removing the contents of his backpack. He took out a red-and-white checked cloth and put it on the ground beside Laura. Then he began to fill it with an assortment of interesting packages.

"Climbers need fuel." He placed crackers, cheese, dried fruit rolls, and cookies on the cloth.

"All we need now is something cool to drink."

"Never fear. There's a little creek tumbling over the rocks to our left. I know the water here isn't polluted, and I have a couple of collapsible cups. Would you like to go with me to get it, or shall I bring it to you?"

Laura jumped up and took the red cup, leaving him the blue one. "I'd love to see the creek. Lead me to it."

The break was pleasant. As they shared the snacks, Charles pointed out some of the things they could see from the ledge. Laura felt like she was sitting on top of the world even though they weren't at the top of the mountain yet. She saw the intense colors of the leaves all across the vista before them. There were a few houses they could see, but each seemed isolated. Isolation sounded pretty good to her right now. They watched squirrels gathering nuts for winter. In the distance, they saw a herd of deer with a big buck, several smaller bucks, probably ten does, and some fawns that looked like they weren't a year old yet. They heard a sound behind them and turned to see a raccoon sitting on a rock a little bit higher than they were. It was working with something in its paws.

"I had never noticed how much like hands a raccoon's paws are," Laura whispered. She didn't want to scare it away.

After they had rested about twenty minutes, Charles started to reload his backpack. "If we don't start now, we'll never make it to Granny's with any time to spend with her. She would be disappointed."

As they topped the summit, Laura caught her breath. On the other side was the lake, its smooth surface a mirror in which the trees were reflected. Laura was spellbound. Charles didn't intrude, but stood back and let her draw what peace and strength she needed from the beauty of the scene.

"You know, God really knew what He was doing when He created Earth." She finally turned to Charles. "Thank you for sharing this with me."

The climb down to the cabin nestled among the trees on the lakeshore was easy. Laura almost ran. As they approached the cabin, she could see Granny out back taking her wash off the line. She rushed up to Granny and began helping her. Carefully folding the sheets she took off the line, Laura put them in the basket at Granny's feet.

"Land sakes. I never thought I'd have help takin' in my washin'. How did you get here?"

"We came over the mountain this time. I wanted to show Laura our domain in all its autumn glory." Charles lifted the full clothes basket and started toward the cabin.

"I was wonderin' why Chuckie never brought you again. I've been hankerin' to see you. Come in and we'll have some gingerbread. I made it this mornin'."

While Granny was cutting the gingerbread and pouring the apple cider, Laura and Charles took off their backpacks and sat down by the table.

"Why don't we go in the parlor? We don't have to set

in the kitchen."

"Granny, you know this is my favorite part of the house. Laura isn't a visitor today. Let's stay here like family."

The smile that spread across the weathered face lit it up. "Of course, you can set anywhere you want to."

Laura took the paperweight from her backpack and extended it to the older woman. "I want to be considered a part of your big family. Here's a picture of me and my family for your collection."

Granny's smile spread so wide it almost dropped off the sides of her face.

After the three of them had spent a pleasant half hour, Charles went outside to check on things.

"You've got something on your mind. Do you want to tell me about it?" Granny's smile went straight to Laura's heart.

"How did you know?"

"Honey-chile, I know we only been together one other time, but I can tell somethin's botherin' you."

Without hesitation, Laura began to tell Granny about the harrowing experiences with Gerald. It seemed natural to be sharing with this wise mountain woman. The words poured from her heart in a torrent until the whole ugly story was out.

"Now, Honey, you're blamin' yourself for what happened."

"I should have recognized the clues. They were there. Maybe there's something in me that drew him to me."

"There is, but you wouldn't want to change it. He was

drawn by your innocence. You can't take the blame for his sins."

"I know that, but I feel almost dirty. I was falling for his charms. I should have realized what he was. Maybe I'm not a very good Christian."

"I don't believe that for a minute. You're goin' to have to forgive yourself. Jesus forgave you. If there's anything I know about my Jesus, it's that He forgives when you ask Him to."

Laura threw her arms around the white-haired woman and hugged her. "I love you, Granny. You've made me feel so much better."

When Charles came back into the cabin, the grass had been cut, and the sun was quite a bit lower in the west. The women couldn't believe it was so late.

"Granny, do you have anything I need to fix before we go?" When Granny told Charles everything was all right, he began emptying his backpack of extra food. "I brought you some of that cheese you like so much. . .and some crackers to go with it."

"You're such a sweet boy, Chuckie." Granny raised her wrinkled hand to caress his cheek. Laura saw the love that flowed between them, and she felt blessed to be a small part of the relationship. Charles gave Granny a bear hug and a kiss as he promised to come again soon.

There were tears in Granny's eyes as Laura and Charles started back up the mountain trail. She waved to them until she couldn't see them any more, then went into the house hoping that Charles and Laura would soon fall in love. She knew they would be good for each other.

The climb up this side of the mountain was not as hard as the climb up the other side had been. It went fast, and Laura didn't feel as tired when they reached the top. As she looked in what she thought to be the direction of the car, she couldn't find it.

"I don't know which way to go."

"That's okay. I'll go ahead of you." Charles started down the trail, often looking over his shoulder to check on her. Once, just as he looked, Laura's foot caught on the root of a tree, and she pitched forward. Quickly he turned and caught her in his strong arms. He held her trembling body close to his chest, and she could feel his heart beating almost as fast as hers. Was it her fear of a bad fall, or...something else?

In the instant her foot had caught, she had imagined her body tumbling down the mountain and landing in a broken heap at the bottom. She took a breath and relaxed in his arms. He didn't seem in a hurry to let her go. . .and she didn't care. She felt his cheek against her hair, his warm breath stirring the copper tendrils that dangled there. His right hand crept up to cradle her head against the expanse of his chest while his left hand pulled her waist closer to him. His hard muscles warmed her softer flesh. She felt she was where she belonged. She slid her arms around his waist and felt the muscles ripple in his strong back.

When her breathing returned to normal, she tipped her head just enough to see his face. He was peering over the mountains not focusing on anything. When he felt her move, he glanced down. Concern was written all over his face. They were totally unaware of the passage of time as their eyes searched the inner recesses of each other's hearts.

Laura had no idea how long they had stood there. She didn't want the moment to end. His gaze drifted over the contours of her face, then rested on her trembling lips. His face slowly lowered until their lips met. The gentle touch awakened feelings in her she had never experienced before. The things she had felt in other kisses were nothing compared with this explosion of emotion that spread through her body. As the kiss deepened, she didn't resist. She soared far above the clouds that drifted over the mountains, and she knew she was not alone. They swirled together through the infinite reaches of the universe locked in an embrace.

When they finally drew apart, Charles continued to look deeply into her eyes. She swayed. He steadied her, then took her hand and headed down the mountain trail without a word.

By the time they reached the clearing where the car was parked, Laura's backpack was full of beautiful leaves for her bulletin board at school. They also picked up several rocks for a nature center. She took the backpack off and put it in the car, then leaned against the fender and looked around the clearing.

After Charles put his backpack in the car, he stood in front of her. "Are you ready to go home? It'll soon be dark.

Nightfall comes quickly in the mountains."

Laura turned her attention to the man standing so near. She was instantly aware of the muscles beneath the knit shirt he wore. Their strength had sustained her on the trek down the trail to the car, and his tender caresses had blocked out the painful past. She looked into his blue eyes which shimmered in the fading sunlight.

"Yes. Let's go home. I'm tired after so much exertion, but it's a good tired. . .I want to cook supper for you."

"Okay. We'll stop by a store on the way. I'll buy the steaks, if you'll cook them."

fourteen

Laura mentally shook herself near the end of Pastor Jones' sermon. She hadn't heard a word of it because she had been going over the events of the day before. The time she had spent with Charles had proved to be somewhat disturbing. She had enjoyed their hike over the mountains, but the personal interaction had been unsettling. She had felt confused last night when Charles apologized for taking advantage of her on the trail. He told her he was trying to help her deal with the trauma she had experienced with Gerald, not add to her emotional confusion. She knew she could not have been completely mistaken that they had shared the same feelings on the mountain. Maybe she had imagined that he had felt something. Of course, he didn't know that for those few precious hours, the trauma had been blocked out of her thoughts. Now she questioned her part in that. Had she led Gerald on because of some need to be loved? Had that need also drawn that emotional kiss from Charles on the mountain? Had he later regretted it? The questions swirled around in her feverish mind.

"Oh, Lord, help me sort this out." Her silent prayer preceded the spoken prayer of the pastor by only a few seconds. She was glad there was an exit near the choir room door. She couldn't comment on the pastor's sermon when she hadn't heard one word of it.

Rose was standing in the hall waiting for her. "Laura, Susan was supposed to work this afternoon, but she's sick. Could you fill in for her?"

"Of course I will. I was beginning to think I was cheating you. . .getting the suite at a reduced rate. You haven't had me work yet, and I've been there almost two months."

"It's worth the money to know that I have a substitute available. If you'll come when you finish dinner, I'd appreciate it. Ralph was on duty this morning. He agreed to stay until you had eaten. If you want to, you can take your lunch to the front desk. I don't anticipate too much business this early in the afternoon, so you should be able to finish without too many interruptions."

When the night clerk came on at 8:00, Laura was glad. It had been good to have something to do that afternoon, but it had been a little boring because there hadn't been much business. There had been several long stretches with nothing to do but read. She had read everything that was in the lobby. Just as she opened her door, the phone was ringing. Her grandfather wanted to make sure she was okay. . .and that she planned to go to their house for Thanksgiving.

Tuesday afternoon, Joey Brown breezed into her room. He started talking as soon as he opened the door. He had found the car he wanted, and he knew he would have all the money for it by the time he turned sixteen in December. His grandfather had already said he could buy it.

"You know, Miss Bentley, it looks like everything in my life is just about perfect."

"What more do you need to make it perfect?"

"If I get good enough grades to win a full scholarship, I wouldn't want anything else."

Laura knew Joey meant what he said. He was studying hard, and his grades were getting better. More than that, he was acquiring good study habits. They would help him when he got to college.

Laura woke on Wednesday morning wanting a mushroom omelet, so she went to the restaurant for breakfast. She had tried to duplicate the omelet in her kitchen, but it never tasted as good. When she stepped from the elevator, George was passing by on his way to the restaurant.

"Have you had breakfast?" George asked. After a quick "No", he took her arm and steered her through the door. "Good. You can have breakfast with me."

"Where have you been lately?" Laura quizzed him after they had ordered.

"The case I'm working on takes me out of town a lot. Of course, that isn't all that takes me out of town. I've been seeing as much as possible of Charlene. Our relationship is really getting serious."

"I've prayed that the Lord would close the door on the relationship if she isn't the right one for you."

"I'm glad. I am interested in her, but I only want the

woman God wants for me. She shares our faith in Jesus."
George reached across the table and took Laura's hand in
his. "I'm so glad to have a 'sister' like you. It means so
much having someone I can talk to about important things
like this."

"I know. You've been the brother I have needed, too."
Laura noticed over George's shoulder that Charles was
coming toward them. "Of course, you have a best friend,
too."

"It's not the same. I haven't been able to tell him about
Charlene. I know I should, but I can't yet. Maybe, soon."

Just then Charles pulled out a chair between George and
Laura. "I hope I'm not interrupting anything." He also
hoped his casualness didn't sound forced.

"Of course not," George replied. "We're always glad
to see you, aren't we, Laura?"

"Sure. Where have you been? I haven't seen you in the
cafeteria like I usually do."

Charles looked at the centerpiece on the table as he
replied. "I've had a lot of work to do, so I've been taking
my lunch in my room. . .How have you been?"

"I'm fine. Our excursion on Saturday was a big help. It
helped me put things in better perspective. I'm still
seeking the Lord's direction for a complete healing."
Laura wanted him to look up. She wanted to see the
expression in his eyes.

Before he did, George interjected, "What are you two
talking about? Have I missed something?" He looked
from one to the other.

"I haven't been able to give you the report of what I found out Friday night. You've been out of town. I guess we need to tell you what else happened while we were there...if it's all right with you, Laura." Finally he looked at her, but his eyes had a shuttered look.

Laura nodded her assent. A brother would care without condemning. Again, George took her hand across the table and gave it a squeeze.

When Charles finished the story, George looked from one of them to the other. "I'm so sorry. I had no idea that helping me would hurt you so."

"I'm glad it happened," Laura assured him. "If it hadn't, I might have continued a relationship that would have been so wrong. It hurt me when it happened, but it was God's way of answering our prayers."

Laura left the two men so she could finish getting ready for school. Charles gave George the report on what he had found out at the club.

"Do you have time to talk?" George asked when Charles finished. "I want to tell you something."

"Sure. What are friends for?" Charles could tell George was serious.

"I haven't been able to tell you about this before. It's hard for me to open up about some things...even to a friend as good as you are...I think I'm falling in love—for the first time in my life. She's really special. I'm going to ask her to marry me soon."

Charles felt a growing apprehension. "I'm happy for you." He hoped he sounded more sincere to George than he did to his own ears. "I know I shouldn't have to ask this, but is she a Christian?"

"Of course, I wouldn't even consider a lasting relationship with a woman who doesn't know Jesus."

"I thought so. I just had to be sure." His apprehension hit him in the stomach like a weighted medicine ball.

"I understand. I'm afraid I can't tell you any more right now, but would you be praying for us?"

"Like I say, what are friends for?" Charles again asked as he stood up and reached for his check.

Charles drove slowly to the school, but he didn't get out of his car right away. As he stared unseeing across the valley, he asked himself, "How can I pray for them?"

When he reached his room, he closed the door and went to stand by the windows. He didn't even see autumn exploding around him. His mind was on other things.

The end of October and the first part of November rushed by. Laura was busy with teaching, which had become a real joy. The extra-curricular activities kept her busy, too. Charles was a good sponsor for FTA and made her feel like she was making an important contribution. She had as much input as he did, and she appreciated that. His other behavior around her was disturbing. He was friendly, but an aloofness now shaded his eyes. She began to wonder if he could possibly be the same man who had spent that glorious afternoon on the mountain with her. Had she imagined the passion in their embrace? She tried to get the memory of those breathless spiraling minutes out of her mind, but it returned frequently. Too many mornings she awoke with the feeling his lips had branded on hers.

Joey Brown was continuing to make excellent progress. His grades in all subjects were improving because of his new study skills. In fact, the whole school had high spirits lately. For the first time in over twenty years, their football team was having a winning year. They went through the play-offs with flying colors. The championship game was scheduled the week after Thanksgiving. It was hard to get most of the students to study, but not Joey. He cared about the championship, but he cared more about his future.

The day before the Thanksgiving holidays, the PTA served the teachers a special luncheon in Teachers' Lounge. When Laura went on her lunch period, Joyce, Charles, and Beverly Young were the only teachers there. They were sitting at one of the tables talking, so Laura filled her plate and joined them.

"I want to thank you for the extra work you're doing with Joey Brown," Beverly said. "His English grade has gone from a C to a B. If he continues to improve, he could easily have an A by the end of the semester."

Laura wanted no other reward from teaching. Her first year was a success in her own heart because of the success with that one special student.

fifteen

The trip to North Little Rock went much faster than the trip to the Ozarks had in August. Because she was enjoying finding her favorite landmarks, she reached the gate to her grandparents' farm quickly. Before she was halfway up the drive, the door was thrown open by a tiny gray-haired dynamo, who waved enthusiastically as Laura approached the house.

"Grandmother, how wonderful you look!"

"Let me look at you, Laura." Tears were streaming down the wrinkled cheeks. "We have a lot of talking to do, young lady."

"There'll be plenty of time for that while I'm here. Where's Grandfather?"

As if in answer to her question, a tall man with flowing white hair came around the corner of the house. The old man's eyes twinkled. "How's my favorite granddaughter?"

"Your only granddaughter, you mean." Laura couldn't help giggling at the joke she shared with her grandfather every time they were together.

A feeling of contentment swept over Laura as it always did when she entered the house. Her eyes sought and found her favorite things in the familiar rooms. One whole wall was covered with photographs spanning four generations of Laura's family. Laura thought of that wall as the gallery of her heritage.

"I hope you didn't stop to eat before you got here."

"You know, I've missed your cooking while I've been away."

"You do look like you've lost a little weight. Haven't you been eating right?" The genuine concern in her grandmother's eyes kept Laura from being upset.

"Yes. I've been careful to eat well-balanced meals, but no one can cook like you."

After a time of catching up with each other, her grandfather went to the barn to check on a cow that had not been feeling well.

"Do you need to talk to me alone, or do you want to share with both of us?"

"I've been trying to decide. That's why I haven't brought it up yet. I think I'll wait until Granddaddy returns. I know you don't keep secrets from him. He might just as well hear it from me, too."

Laura's grandfather was sitting in front of the fire. She ran across the braided rug and threw her arms around him.

"I've been wanting to talk to the two of you about something important. It's been hard for me to find the words to start."

Laura took a long time telling what had happened in her relationship with Gerald. She didn't want to get any of the details wrong, and she didn't want to place all the blame on him. When she was finished, she gathered her knees up to her chest and lowered her head to rest on them. The three of them sat in silence for a few minutes.

"I never wanted my child or grandchild to have to experience the darker side of life." The voice that broke the stillness was strong and full of compassion. "I know this hasn't been easy, but life isn't easy. I know the evil that can lurk in the heart of a man who doesn't know the Lord. I haven't always known Him myself."

"Laura, when did this last incident take place?" her grandmother interjected when he paused.

When Laura told her, she continued, "The Lord impressed on me to go into deep intercessory prayer for you that day. I didn't know why at the time. I felt it was something serious, but after about 10:00 that night, I felt a release."

Laura had known the Lord loved her, but to have her grandmother pray for her when she was facing such difficulties affirmed that deep love.

Thanksgiving Day was glorious. The sun shone brightly, and the air was cool. The day was spent feasting and remembering other holidays. It was a vacation that renewed her before her return to work.

sixteen

When Laura entered the dining room at the Lodge on Monday morning, she saw George's welcoming smile. "I hope you don't mind if I have breakfast with you."

"I was hoping you would be here this morning." His eyes held a special sparkle. "I want to tell you about my Thanksgiving holiday."

After Laura ordered her omelet, she gave him her undivided attention. He had spent the holiday weekend with Charlene, and the time was fast approaching when he was going to ask her to be his wife.

"No wonder your eyes are gleaming." Laura's enthusiasm was genuine. She reached across the table and gave his hand a squeeze. "I'm so happy for you."

Just then George looked up and greeted Charles as he approached their table. Laura put both her hands in her lap as Charles sat down between them.

"How was your Thanksgiving, Charles?" Her quick question seemed to catch him off guard.

"I didn't interrupt anything, did I?" He looked from one to the other.

"Of course not. How was your Thanksgiving?" George repeated the question.

"I spent it on the mountain with Granny. There were

some repairs I wanted to do to her cabin. I shot a wild turkey, and she cooked it for Thanksgiving dinner."

The days between Thanksgiving and Christmas were hectic—filled with activities at both school and church. Laura threw herself into each one with a fervor.

"I don't know how you can keep up with all you're doing." Renae sat holding Josie on her lap. "Your energy level must be higher than mine."

"I'm just not loaded with emotional entanglements and guilt now," Laura laughed as she warmed her hands at the fireplace. She had shaken the snow off on the porch, but the cold seemed to cling. "You use plenty of energy chasing after the little angel in your lap. I guess you're glad when she takes her naps."

"Yes, but she usually does it in her bed, not in my lap. I don't get much done this way."

"That's all right. Sometimes you need to just sit and hold your child. She'll be gone soon enough. . .I'm glad this was the last day of school before the Christmas holidays. I'm ready for another break."

"And I'm glad you agreed to have Christmas with us this year. So is Mother."

"I only agreed to stay here if the two of you didn't go to any trouble."

"Mother is in her element. She loves Christmas, and she loves sharing it with as many people as possible. It's been so many years since we were together at Christmas, she's going all out. . .but it isn't trouble to her."

Just then, a horn began to honk outside the house. At first the two women ignored it. After a minute, Laura looked out the window to see what was happening. "Do you know anyone who drives a yellow Chevrolet?"

"No. Why?"

"There's one in the driveway behind my car. I think that's where the honking is coming from. I'll go check." Laura opened the door. Joey Brown jumped from the driver's seat of the car and hurried up the walk.

"Miss Bentley, I wanted you to see my car. I picked it up after school today. How do you like it?"

"It's really a beauty, Joey. Whoever owned it must have taken very good care of it. It looks almost new."

"Would you like to take a ride in it? Oh, I guess I shouldn't have asked that. After all, you're my teacher."

"I hope I'm also your friend. I'd love to go for a spin."

Joey even offered to let her drive. "I want you to see how it runs," he added as he handed her the keys.

When they returned, Laura agreed he had "gotten a really good deal."

As Laura put the finishing touches on her makeup before the singles' class Christmas party, she couldn't help being glad that George had insisted on picking her up. She wasn't particularly fond of driving in a snowstorm, but she was glad they hadn't called the party off. The last day of school before the holidays had left her keyed up. She surveyed her makeup with a critical eye. Then, she donned her party clothes.

Before George started the car to take her to the church, he drew a tiny blue jeweler's box from the pocket of his coat. When he opened it, she gasped. "It's beautiful. Is this Charlene's Christmas present?"

"If I can wait until Christmas to give it to her."

"It's only four days away."

"I know, but I'm going there Sunday. I don't know if I'll be able to wait another two days."

"I'm sure she won't care if she gets an early Christmas present."

The room was full when they entered, and Laura took her fruitcake to the decorated table on the other side of the room. George was looking for Charles. When he found him, he took him out in the hall.

"You remember my mentioning a special girl to you?" When Charles nodded, he continued. "I want to show you what I got her for Christmas." He again drew the tiny box from its hiding place and opened it.

"Does she know?"

"No. It's a surprise."

"Are you sure she'll accept it?"

"Almost. We've become very close these last two months."

"Well, I can't do anything but wish you the best. You know you're my best friend. All I want is for you to be happy."

When the two men returned to the room, they saw a smiling redhead cross the room toward them. When she reached them, she linked her arms with both of them and propelled them to the refreshment table. "I know you two like to eat. Why were you hiding in the hall?"

"No reason," George laughed. "Lead me to the food."

When they reached the end of the heavily laden table, Charles had only a couple of cookies on his plate. Laura teased him about watching his weight. He told them he had developed a headache. He was going home to try to get rid of it. George offered to drive him, but he refused.

Sunday dawned clear and bright, with the sun reflecting off the white, puffy blanket that had gently drifted over the landscape during the night. On the way to church, Laura reveled in the jeweled brilliance. She was glad George had insisted on putting the chains on her tires before he left yesterday, because she felt much safer on the winding road to the church. Since Christmas music had always been her favorite, she was looking forward to the Christmas cantata that morning. How she loved to sing about the Baby Who had come to save the world!

Entering the door of the church, she unconciously scanned the gathering crowd for Charles. She wondered if he were feeling better. As she looked at each usher, she was disappointed, and her heart sank. What was going on? She was so happy when she left the Lodge. How could her mood change so quickly? She went into the sanctuary for a time of meditation before the choir gathered to prepare for the morning service.

"Lord, I love you so much. I was so full of joy. What's

the matter with me?"

As she sat in silence, a question slipped into her mind. What exactly happened when you felt the peace slip away? Was that a question from the Lord? What had happened? Each time she had looked at an usher's face and had seen that he was not Charles, she had felt disappointed. Why? In the silence an answer came. She loved Charles. When had that happened? Could it be that the Lord approved of that love? Joy bubbled inside her until it overflowed and ran down her cheeks. The world took on a new sparkle, even more brilliant than the crystal snow outside. What could she do about her newfound love? Nothing. She would just have to ask the Lord for patience.

Laura had even more to praise her Savior for as the choir sang the beautiful story of the season. After the service, the choir director told her that he had never heard her sing as well as she did that morning—especially her solo, "My Soul Does Magnify the Lord."

On Monday, Laura finished her shopping and wrapped her gifts. Her eyes looked expectantly at every male face she encountered. Each time, she was disappointed, but her heart still sang. She knew she loved a wonderful, Godly man. She knew he didn't love her. . .but that could change.

Because she wasn't going to be with her family, she had offered to work the desk at the Lodge on Christmas Eve. She wanted to give everyone else a chance to be with their loved ones. When she closed the desk at 10:00, it would remain closed until the day after Christmas.

Christmas Day proved to be worth the extensive preparations. After a return trip around the table in the evening, the adults were discussing past Christmases, when the doorbell rang. Laura brightened when Charles entered the snug den.

"What did I interrupt?" Charles leaned closer to the fire to warm his hands.

"We were talking about all the stories that mean Christmas to us. Laura said her favorite is 'The Gift of the Magi' by O. Henry." Joe looked from Charles to Laura. "She said it shows what Christmas means to her. . .the spirit of giving instead of getting."

"I wonder if Laura would be willing to cut that beautiful, long, red hair to buy a gift for the man she loved?" Ralph looked at her, expecting an answer.

Laura turned to look at Ralph. "Of course, I'd give anything for the man I love."

She spoke with the conviction of a woman in love. Only Joe saw Charles wince when she made the declaration. He had suspected for some time that Charles was in love with Laura, but for the life of him, he couldn't understand why two people who loved each other didn't even look at each other.

Charles swung his gaze to Laura's left hand. No ring! Feeling the scrutiny he had been going through, he looked at Joe. He tried to hide the questions that tumbled around in his head. He guessed by the knowing look in Joe's eyes that he hadn't been successful. Joe slipped out the door toward the kitchen as the pleasant chatter resumed. Charles soon followed.

Renae, who hadn't been ignorant of the undercurrent, asked, "Laura, I hate to bother you, but would you see if the coffeepot has finished perking again? The carafe is almost empty."

"Sure." Laura, who had been peering into the depths of the light show in the fireplace, didn't realize the two men were already in the kitchen.

"Do you know what's going on between Laura and George?" Laura heard Charles ask as she stood transfixed in the doorway. His back was turned so he did not see her.

"What makes you think something is going on between George and Laura?" Joe inquired, as he looked past Charles into Laura's startled face.

"He told me he has fallen in love, and. . .well, they've been together a lot. I've seen them holding hands in the restaurant at the Lodge. He even showed me the ring he is going to give her for Christmas," he blurted.

"Did he mention Laura's name?" Now Joe was puzzled.

"No."

"Are you sure it's Laura?"

"I don't know what to think. She doesn't have the ring on. He said he would have a hard time waiting until Christmas to give it to her. Do you think she turned him down?"

"Charles, I knew something had been bothering you. I couldn't figure out what until tonight. Why didn't you talk to me?"

"I couldn't talk to anyone. I couldn't tell even you that

I was falling in love with my best friend's girl."

Charles must have heard Laura's gasp, because he wheeled to face her.

"Did you honestly think George is in love with me?"

"What else could I think?"

"So that's why I felt a wall between us. I was so confused. I knew you felt something for me after what happened on the mountain."

In two strides Charles crossed the room and enfolded her in his embrace. One hand pressed her head to his shoulder as the other arm pulled her waist as close as he could. "I've been struggling with my feelings for you since I realized you and George spent so much time together." He breathed the fragrance of her hair, then brushed his lips against it.

Laura raised her head. "George and I have become very special friends. We love each other, but just as brother and sister. He's been talking to me about Charlene. He showed me the ring, too. He left Sunday to be with her family for Christmas."

His arms held her even closer to his chest. She could hear the drumbeat of his heart as it throbbed in time with hers.

"How could I have been so foolish?"

His look of love filled the longing in her heart. The first touch of their lips was gentle—almost shy. Shivers ran up Laura's spine. At her involuntary tremor, his arm tightened until their bodies were pressed closer together. His lips trembled slightly as he pledged his love.

Laura returned his ardor enthusiastically as the shiver was replaced by the sudden warmth that coursed through her veins. They were locked in a world all their own. When their lips reluctantly parted, they relaxed in the embrace.

"Is it safe to come in yet?" Joe's laughing voice drew their attention to the kitchen door.

Charles took Laura's hand as they moved apart. "Evidently I've been under a number of wrong impressions."

"Well, it looks like everything is straightened out now." Joe put his arm around Laura as he put his hand on Charles's shoulder. "And I'm glad."

"What are you glad about?" Renae looked from one to the other as she entered the kitchen. "If it's what it looks like, so am I."

"Are you ready to join us, or do you need more time?" Joe took Renae's arm. "Why don't you come into the den when you are ready?"

"How did he know I wasn't through talking to you?" Charles's laugh thrilled Laura just as it had the first time she had heard it. "You know what this means to me, don't you? I want you to become my wife. Will you, Laura?"

"Yes." Laura nodded.

"I wish I had a ring to slip on your finger right now."

"Charles, you're all I want. I'll marry you any time you say."

"Don't tempt me, or I'll take you to the Justice of the Peace tonight."

"I know we wouldn't feel married unless we were

married by a minister, but your idea sounds wonderful right now. Especially if you're going to kiss me like you did a while ago."

"Thanks for the suggestion." Charles' eyes sparkled. He locked her in his well-muscled arms and smothered her with a burning kiss, leaving her light-headed and smiling.

"Maybe we had better join the others for our own good." Charles kept his arm around her waist as he steered her into the den.

Laura wondered if anyone besides Joe and Renae would notice anything. That had been a silly thought. The minute they entered the den, they were deluged with congratulations and questions. They announced the engagement but couldn't give any details about the wedding.

In the middle of the uproar, the doorbell rang. Joe hurried to answer it and was surprised to see the sheriff. "Is Miss Bentley here tonight by any chance?"

"Yes, Sheriff. Come on in." Joe stepped back.

"I don't want to interrupt your Christmas. If I could just see Miss Bentley here in the hall, I would appreciate it."

Not wanting to release his hold on her, Charles accompanied Laura to the hall. "What seems to be the trouble, Sheriff?"

"I'm glad you're here with Miss Bentley, Charles. There's been a terrible accident. Joey Brown has been killed." Laura's face paled as she lay her head weakly on Charles's shoulder. "His grandparents are in no shape to identify the body. They said Miss Bentley is close to him.

I hate to ask you this, but would you be willing to come to the sight of the accident?"

"How did it happen?" Laura was able to whisper.

"He had gone to town to take some food to a needy family, and he was on his way home. When he topped the rise just before the War Eagle bridge, a flat-bed truck was stopped in his lane with no lights on. He ran under it. I'm afraid it sheared the top off his car."

Laura swayed in Charles' strong grasp.

"Why was the truck stopped in the road?" Charles asked.

"The driver was stoned. He thought he had pulled off the road before he went to sleep. They found drug paraphernalia along with a plastic bag of white powder in the glove compartment of the truck."

Laura sobbed against Charles's chest until her body was almost limp.

"I'll go with you, Sheriff," Charles offered. "Laura, you stay with Joe and Renae. I'll be back as soon as I can."

At the funeral, Laura sat with Joey's grandparents since they didn't have any other family. It was all too much. She had lost her family in a car wreck. She had been attacked by drug users. Now Joey was killed in an accident by a drug user. During the service, Laura was strong for the sake of the grieving grandparents. As they sat there, she couldn't help thinking about the day, less than a week ago, when she had driven the happy boy's car around the block.

seventeen

George came home from his holiday with glowing reports of his engagement. He and Laura were having breakfast the first day of school in January. Just as he finished relating all the developments in his relationship with Charlene, Charles walked in. When he reached their table, he leaned down and kissed Laura hard on the mouth. George's eyes almost popped out of his head.

"Have I been missing something?" His eyes danced as he looked at his two best friends.

Charles reached into his pocket and took out a tiny jeweler's box. When he opened it, he slipped a diamond surrounded by emeralds on Laura's finger.

"Does this tell you something?" he laughed.

Laura couldn't take her eyes off the beautiful ring. "How did you know I love emeralds?"

"Don't all redheads?"

While Laura went to her suite to get her coat and purse, George and Charles discussed the other events that had just transpired.

"The wreck that killed Joey Brown has the whole town in an uproar," Charles informed his friend.

"I'm sure it does. I'm glad we're almost ready to make an arrest. We're going for the man who is the top drug dealer in this part of the country. We're almost sure we know who he is. We're waiting for one report. Then we'll move in."

"The whole county will rest easier then. If you're able to get a conviction, maybe the people will be better able to handle Joey's death. You know how well liked he was."

"You know, Charles, I am glad you and Laura have finally realized you were made for each other. She needs your strength now. . .and she may need it more in the coming days."

Just then, Laura returned. "Are you ready to go to school now?" Her smile was for Charles alone.

The first day of school was hard. The tragic events since Christmas had cast a pall over the whole student body. The teachers had all known Joey whether he was in their classes or not, so they were not immune to the depression that had settled over the school. Laura was glad when the last class was over. Everyone knew how she had been helping Joey. Almost everyone in the building had stopped by her room sometime during the day. She was so emotionally drained when the last of the students left her room, that she put her head on her desk and cried. That's how Charles found her.

"We're going for a drive in the mountains." He eased her from her chair and held her in his strong arms before he helped her into her coat and led her to his car.

As they drove through the pass out of town, Laura immersed herself in the scenery sweeping past her. She had been so busy with activities before Christmas that she hadn't taken the time to enjoy her surroundings. Now she looked over the snow-clad mountains. Very quickly,

George turned into one of the many lookout points along the highway.

The blanket of white was a perfect backdrop for the skeleton trees reaching their bony arms toward the sky. The scattered evergreens were tufted with the same white. Because the sun was shining in the blue expanse above, the snow crystals glistened like diamonds across the countryside. As Laura realized that, she glanced down to the gems on the third finger of her left hand and smiled.

"What brought the sunshine to your face?" The gentle masculine voice caressed her.

"I never got a chance to thank you for my ring. You know that wasn't the most romantic spot to get it. . .And it wasn't very private." The laughter in Laura's voice brought a chuckle to Charles's throat. He slid his arm around her and gently pulled her closer to him. She gladly snuggled her shoulder into the curve of his arm as she dropped her head onto his shoulder.

"I'm glad your shoulders are broad and strong. I think I'm going to need your strength."

"That's what I'm here for," he murmured softly near her neck. Laura closed her eyes and rested for the first time all day. They sat in silence for several minutes.

"We need to discuss a wedding some time. How about now?" His lips moved from her ear to her forehead. Gentle kisses stroked her forehead and wandered down her cheek until she tilted her head to receive them. When his lips finished the journey to hers, the touch was no longer gentle, but hungry. Then as they descended the column of her neck to the hollow at the base of her throat, the whole world was blotted out.

"I've been wanting to do that for a long time. It's been torture to look at the throbbing in your throat and not be able to kiss it." His warm breath tickled as it awoke a response in Laura, and she reluctantly pulled away from the kiss.

"If we're going to talk, we had better start while we still can."

"I believe you're right." He caressed her head against his shoulder. "When do you think we ought to get married?"

"Now is not a good time to ask me. I can't think clearly after that. I would almost say tonight."

"My sentiments exactly."

Laura straightened up and pulled a little away from the embrace. "Charles, let's be realistic."

"All right, Darling. How soon can you be ready for a wedding? Could you possibly be ready some time this month?"

"I don't think so. I would like to, but we need to have a nice church wedding for my grandparents. I'm all they have left."

"I understand. How long will that take?"

"I want a simple wedding, don't you? We could put it together by the middle of next month. Will that be soon enough?"

"Not soon enough for me, but I can live with it. Would you like to be married on Valentine's Day?"

Laura melted against Charles. "How romantic. . .Yes, I'd like that very much. I think Valentine's Day is on Thursday this year."

"Maybe Mr. Tounsend would let us get substitutes for

that Thursday and Friday. That would give us a three-day honeymoon, anyway. Then we could go on a real trip in the summer." As Charles drew her mouth to his, Laura was gripped by a yearning so strong she could hardly breathe. How could she ever wait until Valentine's Day? She would, of course, because God had directed her every step to the man who now held her in his arms.

Charles turned toward her and took both of her hands in his. "Darling, let's pray together before we go home."

Laura loved the sound of Charles's voice as he spoke to the Master. "Lord, we know You brought us together, and Your plan is for us to establish a Christian home. We thank You for that. We also thank You for the deep love You are establishing in our lives, and the plan You have for men and women to be able to express their love to each other in a special physical way. Lord, our love is deep, and our physical attraction is very strong. We ask You right now to help us control our desires until after the ceremony uniting us in Your sight. Help us recognize Your leading and follow Your directions. Thank You, Lord. Amen."

He opened his eyes and placed a soft kiss on Laura's waiting lips.

When Laura and Charles arrived at the restaurant in the Lodge for dinner, they were surprised to see George pacing in front of the door.

"I wanted to be the one who told you. I know it's already all over town, so I hoped I could catch you before anyone else did." His intense expression disturbed Laura.

"Tell us what?" Charles exclaimed. "What happened?"

"Just calm down. Let's sit in the back corner booth, and

I'll tell you. It isn't anything to get upset about. I just wanted to be the one to tell you."

Laura noticed that every eye in the place followed the three of them to the back booth. "Now, tell me before I burst." She leaned across the table toward George.

"We arrested 'Mr. Big' in the drug ring today." George paused.

"That's wonderful." Laura let out an audible sigh. "We're not upset about that. We're glad."

"I wanted to be the one to tell you who he is."

"Is he someone we know?" Charles's expression told George he had already guessed.

"Yes. . .It's Gerald Eads."

Laura felt like the wind had been knocked out of her. She turned her stricken face to Charles, who put his arm around her and pulled her to him. She couldn't stop shaking. George reached across the table and took her hands.

"I'm sorry, Laura. I know this is hard on you. This is one reason I was glad the Lord put you and Charles together. It would have been harder on you if you had found out and had no one to lean on."

"I suppose everyone in town knows. I saw all the stares as we walked across the restaurant."

"Yes, Laura. In a small town where feelings are running high because of the death of Joey Brown, it would be impossible to keep it quiet. Gerald is a hometown boy, too."

"They all know I dated him for a while."

"Don't worry, Darling. They also know you and love you." Charles's voice was soothing. "They won't connect you with him now. You're wearing my ring. Most people won't think anything anyway, and the others don't count."

"That's right, Laura," George agreed. "Mr. Tounsend has talked to me about it. He was worried about your reaction. He knew you would feel like this, and he wanted to do what he could to keep you from having any problems. I think most of the town will feel just like he does."

"I certainly hope you're right."

eighteen

Because the D. A.'s people had done their homework—
and because of the emotional nature of the case—it came
to trial quickly. Gerald was a hometown boy, so feelings
were stronger than they would have been if he had been an
outsider.

Laura hadn't planned on going to any of the trial, but
George and Charles thought it would be better if she did.
When she entered the courtroom, Gerald's eyes immediately met hers. How could she have been attracted to him?
He looked different from the man she had spent so much
time with. How could a man change so much? It reminded
her of the scripture in II Timothy 3 about the men of the
world who lead women astray. She thanked the Lord for
saving her from a deep entanglement with a man like that.

All the excitement about the trial filled most of January
and spilled over into February. Everywhere people were
talking about it. When the verdict was brought in, Gerald
was convicted. The D. A.'s office had not left even one
loophole for him to slip through. When the sentence was
handed down for a long prison term, the town heaved a
collective sigh of relief.

Agitation about the trial couldn't dampen the excitement

of the wedding. Laura hadn't realized that there were so many details for even a small wedding. They were going to be married in the church they both attended. Each member of the church was also part of their extended family. Like a big family, various people came to them and asked to be a part of this most important celebration of their love in Jesus.

The last two weeks before the wedding were hard for both Charles and Laura. It was hard to keep the students interested in their subjects when they were in class. Of course, both of them made the effort, but sometimes the classes wandered off the subject. Mr. Tounsend gave the two of them Wednesday off, as well as Thursday and Friday.

Laura's grandparents arrived Tuesday evening, so she was able to spend the day before the wedding with them. They helped with the last-minute details. That night, Charles took the three of them out to dinner at the restaurant at the lookout.

As Laura started down the aisle on her grandfather's arm, she was oblivious to the kaleidoscope of color surrounding her. Her eyes were drawn to the compelling gaze of the man she loved. Her eyes never left his on the long walk down the aisle. His eyes spoke volumes of his deep love, commitment, and desire for her.

"I, Charles. . .take thee, Laura. . ."

Yes, she had truly come home to her heart.

A Letter To Our Readers

Dear Reader:

In order that we might better contribute to your reading enjoyment, we would appreciate your taking a few minutes to respond to the following questions. When completed, please return to the following:

Karen Carroll, Editor
Heartsong Presents
P.O. Box 719
Uhrichsville, Ohio 44683

1. Did you enjoy reading *Home to Her Heart?*
   ☐ Very much. I would like to see more books
      by this author!
   ☐ Moderately
      I would have enjoyed it more if _____

   _____

2. Are you a member of *Heartsong Presents*? Yes   No
   If no, where did you purchase this book? _____

   _____

3. What influenced your decision to purchase
   this book? (Circle those that apply.)

Cover	Back cover copy
Title	Friends
Publicity	Other _____

4. On a scale from 1 (poor) to 10 (superior), please rate the following elements.

___Heroine   ___Plot

___Hero   ___Inspirational theme

___Setting   ___Secondary characters

5. What settings would you like to see covered in *Heartsong Presents* books?

_____

_____

6. What are some inspirational themes you would like to see treated in future books?_____

_____

_____

7. Would you be interested in reading other *Heartsong Presents* titles?   Yes   No

8. Please circle your age range:

| Under 18 | 18-24 | 25-34 |
| 35-45 | 46-55 | Over 55 |

9. How many hours per week do you read? _____

Name _____

Occupation _____

Address _____

City _____ State _____ Zip _____

······ Hearts♥ng ······

Great Inspirational Romance at a Great Price!

Heartsong Presents books are inspirational romances in contemporary and historical settings, designed to give you an enjoyable, spirit-lifting reading experience. You can choose from 52 wonderfully written titles from some of today's best authors like Veda Boyd Jones, Linda Herring, Janelle Jamison, and many others.

HEARTSONG PRESENTS TITLES AVAILABLE NOW:

(If ordering from this page, please remember to include it with the order form.)

·········Presents·········

ABOVE TITLES ARE $2.95 EACH